Delusio Dreams: a short story collection

by

Maria Savva

Published by:
Rose and Freedom Books
P.O. Box 55285
London N22 9EU
England, U.K.

Cover photos by © Martin David Porter
http://www.facebook.com/MartsArtsPhotography

A catalogue record of this book is available from the British Library

ISBN: 978-0-9564101-8-4

Acknowledgements:

Thank you to my beta readers for your invaluat for finding and helping to eradicate those drea and your suggestions for improving the book, a helped me considerably!

Michael Radcliffe
Darcia Helle
Julie Elizabeth Aldridge
Laura Smith
Calum McDonald
Geoffrey D West
Stuart Ross McCallum
Marina Savva

***

Thanks also to Martin David Porter of Mart's Photography, for the perfect cover photos http://www.facebook.com/MartsArtsPhotogra

Contents:

*Originally published in the BestsellerBound Short Story Anthologies Vols. 1-4
**Originally published in Writers' News Magazine, Sept. 2008 (Prize winning story)

Delusion and Dreams - Part I

She is wearing the blue suit today. Yesterday she wore the black one. Her hair's a bit unkempt. Is someone else in the flat? Did he just run his hands through her hair as she was leaving? No. I would have seen him go in. No one went in there last night. Only her. She looks at me as she walks by. Smiles. Such a friendly girl. She doesn't remember me.

Twenty years ago, she would have said hello to me. We used to go to the same college. We were studying Economics; A-level. Such a clever girl; pretty and clever. We never got to know each other but I used to look forward to seeing her every Tuesday and Wednesday... or was it Wednesday and Thursday? I can't remember; so many years have come and gone since those days. She wore her hair shorter then. I sat at the back of the classroom. I used to love watching her. I still do.

Last year, I moved here. After I split up with Elyse, my wife of fifteen years. I never loved Elyse. She got pregnant soon after we started dating, so I married her. Turns out the child isn't even mine. She always had affairs. For ten years I thought Daniel was my son, but then his real dad turned up and we went through the whole paternity dispute. She lied to me right up until the last minute. I should have known he wasn't mine. My eyes are brown, so are Elyse's. Daniel's eyes are blue. His dad's eyes are blue too.

Jessie's eyes are blue. I often used to think that if Jessie and I had a child, its eyes would be blue, like Daniel's. I used to fantasise that Daniel was the child I had with Jessie... whenever Elyse left me alone with the child... when she was off having her affairs. I always wished Daniel could be mine and Jessie's, but he's not even mine.

Elyse has been living with Eric since we divorced: Eric is Daniel's real dad. She's pregnant again. I never did get her pregnant, but he moves in with her and two months later she's expecting another baby. At least Daniel will have the brother or sister he's always wanted. Part of me can't help but wish that the child Elyse is expecting isn't even Eric's... that she's had another affair and the child will be that of a stranger, and Eric will be bringing it up as his own. That would be some kind of karmic payback, wouldn't it?

Sometimes, I follow Jessie to work. I try to keep my distance so that she doesn't see me. I want to approach her and tell her who I am. Under this beard, she would never know me. After the years that have passed between us, she's probably forgotten what I look like without the beard, anyway; and I used to look so different then, as a teenager, before life took away my sparkle. I swear I don't recognise the person looking back at me in old photographs of myself. Not that I have those photographs anymore. Elyse kept the house in the divorce, and everything in it.

When I dream, I imagine that if I approach Jessie and tell her who I am, she will tell me that she has always liked me too, like as if we are soul mates, or something; then we'd move into her flat as a couple.

I haven't seen her with another man. She lives alone. Every day, when she returns from work, I brace myself, worried that this will be the night she returns home with a man. I've checked the fingers on her left hand, she's not wearing any rings. I've been watching her now for three months.

She smiles at me because she sees me every day. I am a familiar face now. Maybe as time goes by she'll say hello, then we can talk, then she'll remember me... maybe then we will get together.

I came here because I knew she lives here. If I was going to be alone, at least I'd be able to see her each day. I never forgot her, all the time I was married to Elyse. It was always Jessie. She has always been my true love.

I took a bus trip with her, once. I can't remember where we were going. Some kind of college open day, a careers fair, something like that. We happened to arrive at the bus stop at the same time, so we agreed to travel together. We talked about what we wanted to do when we left college. I said something stupid like 'I want to work in a bank'. I have no idea why I said that... I have never wanted to work in a bank.

Jessie said she wanted to be a lawyer. She works at the local council offices. I'm not sure what she does there. Maybe she's a lawyer.

I bumped into Shirley last year; she used to be one of Jessie's friends at college. She's the one who told me where Jessie lives. Our conversation went something like:

'Wow, it's been so long! How many years? Twenty? You haven't changed much.'

I could see in her eyes when she said that last part, she was trying to come up with something polite to say.

'Huh! Yeah, not much,' I replied. 'How did you recognise me?'

'I didn't. I'm married to Phil. Philip Ross. Remember you two were quite close at college?'

'Yeah, we kept in touch for a while after. Phil, hey?' I scanned the room with my eyes. 'Where is he?'

'He had to go to the toilet. Told me to come and chat with you and he'd catch up with us. So, how have you been?'

'Me?' I shrugged, blushing slightly, not really wanting to tell.

'You married?'

'No,' I said. 'I was. It's a long story.' I truly wished I hadn't gone to the college reunion, but I'd been hoping Jessie would be there. 'Do you keep in touch with anyone from college?' I asked. A leading question. I hoped she would say she kept in touch with Jessie.

'Um... not really... only Frances. Remember the girl who had the perm and the round glasses?'

I did remember making her cry with one of my comments, and prayed she was not present.

I nodded, embarrassed.

'She's a real stunner now,' said Shirley. 'I bumped into her about three years ago and we've kept in touch, on and off. She has a hectic life. Lots of kids. Doesn't seem to have much time for a social life, poor girl! She didn't come tonight because she's got baby-minding issues.'

'Oh.' I felt disappointed that she had not mentioned Jessie.

'I did keep in touch with Jessie for a while.'

My ears pricked up. 'Really?'

'Yeah, I haven't seen her for years. Last I heard, she was living in Wood Green. She moved back there when her parents went into an old people's home. She's living in the old flat above the newsagent. Remember that shop?'

I nodded.

'She's still single as far as I know. Never did marry. And such a pretty girl.' Shirley frowned.

Anyway, that's how I found out where Jessie lives.

Once in a while, whenever I collect enough pennies, I go into that shop and buy a chocolate bar. Usually a *Snickers* bar... it used to be called *Marathon*, back in the day, when Jessie's parents owned the shop. I preferred *Marathon*. What does *Snickers* even mean?

She used to live upstairs when we were at college, and I often went into the shop hoping I would see her. I did sometimes. She never saw me. It's odd how you just don't *see* some people. If only she'd known how much she meant to me, maybe then she would have taken more notice. That's probably why she's alone; I'm sure we were meant to be together, but somehow it didn't happen. I was duped into marrying Elyse, to bring up her lover's child. So much time we have wasted, Jessie and I. We could have made each other happy. Now here we are; two lonely people. She smiles at me occasionally, but she doesn't smile a lot. She wears a frown most of the time.

I wonder whether she's lonely, living all by herself. It can't be easy. We're in our mid-thirties now. I've never lived alone. Well, not until after I broke up with Elyse, and only until the money ran out. I can't really say I'm living alone now either; out here on the streets. There's always someone walking about, no matter what time of day or night.

The day I was evicted from my flat I thought the world had ended. I used my last five pound note to come here to be close to Jessie. Sometimes, when she smiles at me, I can tell she feels sorry for me. But I feel sorry for her, too. Maybe one day she'll see that I am the answer to her problems. I could move in with her to keep her company, get out of the cold, and we would both be happy. I just have to try to find the nerve to talk to her. One day I will tell her everything.

Hair Today, Gone Tomorrow

Samuel's head felt cold suddenly, like a breeze had swept over him, but he was indoors, in the pub. From the corner of his eye he noticed something moving. Instinctively, he turned to his right, and observed an object that resembled a grey squirrel flying towards the dart board. Only then did he realise he had walked into the path of a dart. His hand went intuitively up to his head as his eyes fixated on the grey toupee hanging precariously from the dartboard. He felt his scalp and watched helplessly as his wig fell to the floor, still attached to the dart.

The sound of laughter emanating from the vicinity of the bar seemed directed at him; an unintended clown in an inadvertent circus. Daring to turn around, he heard the words: 'That was a bullseye! It's not my fault the old fella got in the way.'

As Samuel looked at the man pointing at him, he felt himself blush. Lowering his head, he walked as quickly as he could towards where the wig had fallen.

As he shuffled over to the dart board, he felt mortified to see a tall man in blue jeans leaning down to pick up the wig. The man grinned as he watched Samuel approach. Samuel felt concerned that this man might start to make fun of the hairpiece or his bald head. Would he give the wig back to him?

To his relief, the man held it out towards him. Whilst handing the wig back to Samuel, he simultaneously ran his other hand through his own thick blond hair. The way Samuel saw it, he may as well have been saying: 'Look at my lovely head of hair; I don't need one of these.'

'Er... thank you,' he said to the young man, in an almost-whisper, then bowed his head and turned to walk away.

Samuel had no time to lose. He was eager to get to the men's room as quickly as possible to replace the wig. He had a date with a young woman this evening, and he wanted to look his best. She didn't know he wore a wig, and he doubted she would even recognise him without it on. They'd only met that very afternoon.

They'd met at the local supermarket. Clare was "young" in his eyes, though in her late forties. He was pushing seventy, but keen to find someone as he had grown tired of living alone. Emelda, his wife of nearly fifty years, had died the year before. She had done everything for him. After her death, he had to teach himself how to do all the things he'd taken for granted, from boiling an egg to using the washing machine; it was all new territory for him. His family—two sons and their wives and children—had done their best to help out in the few months after Emelda died, by cooking meals for him and taking them to his house, but now they'd all drifted back to their own busy lives; he hardly saw them.

The first time Samuel had gone shopping for himself, after his wife died, he accidentally bought cat food instead of tuna. He'd loved the tuna sandwiches that Emelda used to make for him and had tried to make one, but with his failing eyesight, and the misleading packaging, he'd bought a tin of gourmet cat food instead. He was almost tempted to buy the same brand again as it tasted so good, but knew it probably wasn't a good idea.

In fact, when he met Clare in the shop, he'd been dawdling around the pet food aisle debating with himself whether food produced for cats would be suitable for humans. He had also been quite tempted to try the "Kitty Treats". He'd just picked up a packet of the aforesaid biscuits when Clare said, 'My cat Terence doesn't like those, but Ruby's quite keen on them.'

Who's Ruby? he wondered, hoping she was this woman's mother or sister, or daughter... Human. Ideally Ruby was human, as that would give him an excuse to buy a packet for himself. Then he wondered whether it was possible that eating one packet of gourmet cat food could have altered his DNA; like when a spider bit Spiderman... or rather, bit Peter Parker and turned him into Spiderman.

Perhaps I'm turning into Catman? he mused. His mind came up with an image of himself dressed in a cape with a large "C" emblazoned on his chest. His mission would be to rid the earth of mice, and eat as much fish as possible.

'Does your cat like those?' asked Clare, pointing at the *Kitty Treats* in his hand.

He felt like a child caught stealing a packet of sweets, and couldn't help blushing slightly. He coughed and looked down at the bag in his hand, then sheepishly addressed Clare: 'Er... have you ever tried cat food, to test it before you give it to your cat?' he mumbled.

Her eyebrows rose so high, he felt afraid they would escape off the top of her head.

'I would never do that,' she said, screwing up her face; even the suggestion appeared to have left a bitter taste in her mouth. 'Have you ever read the list of ingredients? *Ash* is one of them.' She made a gagging sound. 'And,' she whispered, as if she were worried there were cats around who might hear her and be put off their food, 'I've read that they use the bits of meat that are unfit for human consumption; you know, the bits that have gone off. Cats don't have a problem with that, as you must know, being a cat owner. They eat anything. They eat from dustbins, scraps of food they find on the floor, that sort of thing.'

The room began to sway around him, and he felt the muscles in his stomach loosen and contract; it was all he could do to stop himself throwing up. He put the packet of *Kitty Treats* back on the shelf as if he were handling a radioactive substance. 'B... But surely, in... in the gourmet cat food, they use the best ingredients?' His face contorted, like that of a contestant in a gurning competition; he imagined worms and parasites growing in his stomach as a result of his recent dalliance with feline cuisine. Images of hospital visits, prodding and poking from nurses, and surgeons shaking their heads and declaring him doomed, entered his mind's eye.

Clare looked skyward and tapped her chin, evidently debating what her reply should be. Then she surveyed him with something like sympathy in her eyes; the kind of face a parent might wear when having to explain to a young child that Santa Claus doesn't exist.

Samuel gulped.

'Don't get me wrong,' she said, softly. 'I love my cats. But they're not humans. It really doesn't matter what goes into their food. It ain't gonna harm them.' She flicked her hair over her shoulder and rolled her eyes. 'Hey, they drink dirty water, for God's sake; haven't you seen your cat do that?' She didn't wait for an answer. 'Nothing will happen to them. They've got more defences against bacteria than we have.'

He began to feel quite ill.

'I'm Clare,' she said, holding out a hand.

'Samuel,' he replied. 'But you can call me Sam.'

'Thanks.'

They stood shaking hands, and it appeared that neither of them knew when would be a good time to let go. Then Samuel turned to his left, noticing an elderly woman looking longingly at the products they were blocking with their extended handshake. Clare's eyes followed his. They both let go and giggled. Their eyes met and Clare smiled at him.

The old woman leaned into the space between them and picked up a can of cat food, almost apologetically, then moved away quickly.

At that moment, Samuel became aware of an unspoken attraction between himself and Clare. It had been a year since Emelda died and he'd never imagined he would find someone to replace her romantically, believing he was past all that.

If nothing else, his inadvertent consumption of cat food had brought this woman into his life. He only now began to really look at her. She was quite attractive. Shoulder length brown hair with a sprinkling of grey mixed in. Her green eyes reminded him of Emelda's. She was much younger than him, but he got the impression that it didn't bother her. She appeared to be in her mid to late forties. There were no rings on her fingers.

'It's nice to meet you, Sam,' she said. 'So hard to meet people who love cats as much as I do. They're like a part of the family, aren't they?'

'They are.' He nodded, avoiding her eyes, while recalling a similar conversation he'd had with Emelda many years ago:

'I hate cats,' she'd said.

'So do I,' he'd replied. 'Almost as much as I hate my family.'

That was when his family were against his marriage to Emelda.

'I love cats,' he said, snapping back to the present, aware that he would say anything to see Clare again.

The smile that erupted on her face surprised him; it was as if he'd said: 'I love *you*.'

*

Samuel hastened towards the men's room, but noticed the pub door opening and a woman walking in: Clare. In a panic he placed the hairpiece atop his head as quickly as he could, hoping it wasn't too lopsided.

Clare approached the bar and then turned her head towards him. The hint of a smile was about to break out from her face, but instead, a frown took its place. She walked towards him in slow motion, her eyes fixed on his head, and all he could think about was the wig and what it must look like to make her stare at him in that way. Suddenly, she stopped walking and held her forehead as she turned an odd colour; very pale... almost green.

His attention was distracted as he felt the toupee being pulled off again.

'Sorry, mate; just need to get the dart out,' said the tall young man who had been standing at the bar laughing.

Samuel watched as the man took the hairpiece in his hands and pulled hard to retrieve the dart. Simultaneously,

16

he heard a loud shriek, an almost scream. Samuel twisted around to see Clare's eyes bulging, and then there was a loud thump as she fell to the floor.

About a dozen people had gathered around by now. Samuel couldn't help noticing how many of them were whispering and looking at him and then down at Clare. Were people thinking he could be culpable for her fainting fit?

The uppermost thought in his mind that battled to stay ahead of the thought that people were assuming he'd done something to Clare, was: *Am I that ugly without the wig?* Self consciousness, low self esteem, all the things that had made him purchase the wig in the first place, were now taunting him. He felt naked. He couldn't recall anyone having such a violent reaction to seeing him without a wig.

As the people around her tried to rouse Clare, Samuel began to feel queasy and claustrophobic. He grabbed his toupee back from the man who had come to claim his dart, and exited the pub. An ambulance pulled up outside. He shuddered, feeling that it was somehow his fault, but perplexed that she should have fainted because of him. He walked briskly along the high street, eager to get home as soon as possible.

Ten minutes later, he arrived at his front door, panting after walking at break-neck speed to avoid the possibility of people seeing him and maybe fainting. His speed-walking had the result of drawing more attention to him, however. One man even shouted after him: 'Where's the fire?'; and Samuel almost crashed into an elderly woman pulling a shopping trolley.

As he pushed the front door open, a cat leapt out and sped away, startling Samuel. He had almost forgotten kidnapping (or should that be *kitten-napping*) the neighbours' cat. Catching his breath, he shrugged: *I won't be needing him now, anyway.*

He had lured the cat into his house with a tin of tuna before leaving for the pub. He'd wanted the cat to be there when he got back from the pub with Clare. His plan had gone somewhat awry.

Clare had assumed he owned a cat when they met in the pet food aisle at the supermarket, so he didn't want to disappoint her. Moreover, he didn't want her to know the truth—that he had been there with the intention of buying cat food for himself. He'd planned to pretend that the neighbours' cat, Tabby, was his pet; so had locked him inside. Judging by how quickly he'd escaped, Tabby wasn't too happy about it.

As Samuel entered the house, a foul stench forced him to cover his nose with his hands. The place reeked. Tabby, in frustration, must have sprayed the entire house.

Samuel began to open all the windows, and found himself becoming increasingly short of breath. It often crossed his mind that as he was growing older he could no longer do as much without getting tired. He wondered whether the rush to get home and this excessive exertion in trying to open all the windows may have caused his breathlessness. Then he started sneezing, continuously. Even when he blew his nose, he could not stop sneezing. Soon, breathing became a struggle. He grabbed the phone and dialled 999. After giving basic details to the operator, he passed out.

When he awoke, he found himself in an alien environment, but one that at his age was all too familiar: a hospital ward.

Sitting up in bed, he saw a face he recognised in one of the beds at the far side of the room. His mouth fell open. *Clare.* He wanted to hide so she wouldn't see him, but she was looking in his direction. Pretending he hadn't seen her, he laid back down on the bed, praying she would not faint again as he'd not had time to put on his wig when he got home. Thankfully, this time, she didn't scream.

A couple of minutes later, Samuel felt a presence close to his bed and recognised Clare's perfume; a distinctive floral fragrance. He liked it, which is why he remembered it. He'd noticed it in the supermarket and also in the pub.

'Sam?' she said.

Sighing, he sat up, hoping she would not scream or faint. He kept his eyes down.

'Thank God you're not wearing that frightful wig,' she said, sounding relieved.

He looked up at her, confusion etching many new lines amid the wrinkles on his brow.

She placed a hand on her chest. 'I should explain. I have a fear of wigs. Maliaphobia, it's called. I was hoping we'd bump into each other again, so I could explain why... well, why I reacted like I did.'

'Maliaphobia,' he repeated. The strange word slipped off his tongue without intention.

'Yes.' She blushed slightly. 'Um... If you don't mind me asking, why are you here?'

'Er... I'm not actually sure. I... I think I fainted.'

She laughed. 'Well, it seems that we have more than a love of cats in common!'

He tried to smile, but it turned into a frown as he contemplated the possible reasons why he'd ended up in hospital. Had he been overpowered by Tabby's spray in the house, or could it be he was getting too old for all the running around?

'Maybe we can resume our date when we're released from here.' Clare's voice jolted him from his reverie.

Just then a nurse approached and pulled the curtains around his bed, ushering Clare out as she did so. A doctor appeared and said Samuel had suffered an allergic reaction to something. They wanted to run tests.

When the nurse pulled back the curtains, Samuel noticed a man talking to Clare beside her bed. The man had his back to Samuel, but he knew he'd seen him somewhere before, just couldn't quite place him. Clare was batting her eyelashes at this man, and giggling like a teenager. Samuel frowned and found himself hoping it was just a doctor or nurse, but that seemed unlikely as the man wore jeans and a T-shirt. When he turned around and waved good-bye to her, Samuel saw who he was: the man who had picked up his wig in the pub when it had fallen from the dartboard, and called for the ambulance for Clare. The one with the enviable thick blond hair. Their eyes met.

'You okay, mate?' asked the younger man, looking as though he was about to explode into laughter.

Samuel nodded at him and forced a smile.

The man started laughing but turned away covering his mouth.

What had Clare said to him? And why was he there chatting to her in the first place?

When Samuel and Clare met up for a drink a couple of weeks later to "resume their date", Samuel still felt curious, so he asked her about the man.

'Oh.' She brushed it off with a wave of her hand. 'He helped me when I fainted; came to the hospital with me to make sure I was all right.'

Samuel felt a spark of jealousy, and that's when he realised he was falling for her.

Samuel and Clare became quite close over the next few weeks, meeting for dinner and lunch several times. Samuel had even started to feel comfortable not wearing a wig because she told him he looked 'handsome enough without one.'

One morning he received a letter from the hospital with the results of his allergy tests, which stated he was allergic to cats. *Huh! No wonder I've always hated the little blighters,* he thought. But then a more sombre thought invaded his mind; Clare had two cats—he didn't want this to come between them.

He frowned as he remembered that Clare had invited him to her house for dinner that evening. He didn't want to end up in hospital again, but he didn't want to cancel their date. Cursing his bad luck, he phoned her and suggested they meet at his house instead, pretending he wasn't feeling well enough to travel to hers.

Later that day, she brought him a chicken soup that she had prepared, saying the special recipe had always been a cure-all in her family. They shared a pleasant evening. She fussed over him, wanting to make sure he was okay. He revelled in the attention and realised that in the short time he'd known this woman, he had been happy again. She made him happy. He never thought he would feel that way about another woman after Emelda. When she left that evening, it felt wrong; he wanted her to stay with him. He resolved to ask her to move in with him.

The following day, he booked an expensive restaurant and dressed in his best suit.

As they sat opposite each other in the dimly lit restaurant, he felt a flood of emotion. 'Clare, I think we've been getting on really well,' he said, reaching out and taking her hand.

She smiled at him, but coughed nervously. 'Y... Yes, we have.'

Their eyes met, but she lowered hers quickly.

He couldn't be sure, because of the dim lighting, but thought she was blushing. He found that endearing. 'I'd like to ask you something,' he said.

'Um... it's a bit early for marriage, don't you think?' She pulled her hand away and laughed. 'We've only known each other a couple of weeks.'

Samuel withdrew his hand from the table and leaned back on his chair. He felt slightly offended, but knew that if she thought he was about to propose, it was right she should be reluctant to let him proceed; they hardly knew each other. Trying to compose himself, he smiled at her once more, if less brightly this time.

'No.' He shook his head and giggled, trying to lighten the mood. 'You've got the wrong end of the stick. I wasn't going to propose marriage. I was going to ask whether you'd like to move in with me.'

Her eyes closed briefly, then she picked up her glass of wine and took a sip, obviously contemplating what to say. She avoided his eyes that were fixed on her as he waited for a reply.

Placing the wine glass back on the table, she fidgeted in her chair and appeared uncomfortable. When their eyes met, she was frowning.

'It would make sense,' he said, trying to remain positive. 'We spend a lot of time together, and last night when you were at my house in the evening, it felt so right... like you belonged. Didn't you feel it too?'

Whatever else there was going on in the restaurant appeared to be far more interesting; her eyes kept wandering. He looked around him, but couldn't see anything other than more tables with diners out for a romantic evening. Meanwhile, his romantic evening seemed to be evaporating.

Suddenly she turned to him and took a deep breath before clearing her throat, indicating she had something important to say. 'Look, Sam. I don't think Terence and Ruby would be happy moving out. You know how territorial cats are. And, and... well, maybe your cat wouldn't want them moving in.'

He bowed his head. He'd lied to her when she'd visited for dinner the night before by saying his cat was the outdoors type, and he had even gone as far as setting up a cat bowl and putting a bit of food in it so as to make her believe he had a cat.

'Sorry, Clare... I haven't been entirely honest with you. I don't own a cat. It's a long story... but when we first met and you assumed I did—'

'You lied to me,' she said, almost spitting out the words, as if he'd just told her he'd committed a crime.

'It wasn't lying—'

'Well, it wasn't telling the truth, was it?' she said bluntly.

'If you must know, I'm allergic to cats.'

Her eyes widened.

'So, if you move in with me, you can't bring the cats.' He frowned, knowing how much she loved Terence and Ruby. He'd heard her talk about them so much, he almost felt quite attached to them himself.

'I'm sorry, Sam, I can't move in with you—'

'But it's not my fault I'm allergic to cats!' His mouth fell open. 'Are you going to throw away what we have... wh... what we *could* have... because of a pair of cats? Think about it. If I could—'

'It's not the cats,' she said, shaking her head and appearing solemn. 'I'm afraid I haven't been totally honest with you, either.' She pursed her lips, guilt written on her reddened cheeks. 'I've been seeing someone else.'

'But... but you said you like spending time with me. The other day you said I was the sweetest man you'd ever met... your words—'

She waved her hand to stop him speaking. 'Sam, please understand, I never meant to hurt you, or lie to you.'

'No, but you did!' It was the last thing he'd been expecting to hear. For the past few days he had been imagining her moving in with him and the wonderful times they would enjoy in each other's company. Now his dreams were gone, in the blink of an eye. He could only stare at her and hope this was her idea of a joke. He waited until she spoke again.

'At my age, you have to keep your options open,' she said, while folding and unfolding the white napkin in front of her, focussing on the folding fabric fluttering between her hands. 'I like you, but I think I'm in love with Jake.'

'Jake?'

'Sorry.' She stood up, discarding the napkin as she had discarded his heart. 'I should go.' Pushing the chair nearer to the table, she retrieved her bag from the handle. 'I'm really sorry. Things between Jake and I have kind of blossomed quite quickly.'

'Who the hell is Jake?' Samuel stood up.

She bowed her head then sighed. 'I guess I was kind of wrong to lead you on. I didn't realise how serious you were becoming about us. It's just, with the age gap, I see you more as a father figure.'

She walked away.

Father figure? He was left speechless.

Later that evening he decided to drown his sorrows in the local pub. When he walked in, he saw Clare with Jake. It turned out that Jake was the man who had helped her when she fainted; he of the thick blond hair. He had his arm around her, and winked at Samuel when he saw him. 'All right, mate?' he said.

Samuel took one look at the couple and walked out of the pub.

For the next two weeks, his mood fluctuated from black to grey and colours in between. In an attempt to cheer himself up, he decided to go to Bingo one evening. He and Emelda had often gone to Bingo, so going there now was a way for him to feel closer to her, and try to forget about Clare and his broken dreams.

That evening, he met a woman who was also there alone. Glenda. She told him that she had come to Bingo because she missed her husband who had only recently passed away. She wanted to make new friends. Glenda and Samuel soon became friends.

One evening, a week or two after they'd met, Samuel gave her a peck on the cheek to say good-night.

'Be careful,' she said as he placed his hand on her neck. 'You'll dislodge my wig.' She giggled.

For a moment, Samuel's mind went back to the evening at the pub. He managed a laugh: 'I could tell you a funny story about a dislodged wig.'

But he didn't tell her. He had another idea. 'Where did you get your wig?' he asked.

'Why? Are you thinking of getting one? I wouldn't advise it. I think men look much better with bald heads than toupees. You're fine as you are.'

'No... No, it's not for me. It's for a friend. She's been trying to find a decent wig. Yours is lovely. D'you know, I thought it was real hair.'

'Thank you. Very nice of you to say so.'

'Where did you get it?' he asked again, an evil plan brewing in his head.

'I have a friend who sells them. If you like, I could get some samples for your friend.'

'Yes, please,' he replied, mentally rubbing his hands together. 'I'll give you her address. Perhaps your friend could pop over there with some samples. She'd be delighted to see them. Her name's Clare.'

Happy New Year

'Did you kill Mary Bentley?'

There was an echo in the room so that the "ley" at the end of "Bentley" resounded and joined with the reverberation of Jonathan's cough, which followed almost immediately after the policeman asked the question. Jonathan's cheeks coloured a deep red. Would they assume he was guilty now?

'No,' he said, almost too loudly, trying to make up for what could have been wrongly inferred from his cough.

His answer repeated as an echo. Mocking him.

This was the third time DC Briggs had asked him that particular question: *Did you kill Mary Bentley?* The answer remained the same.

'Mr Graves, we have three witnesses who saw you leave the Great Gull pub on the night of Mary Bentley's disappearance. We have CCTV evidence of you walking along the high street with her, towards the forest where her body was discovered. It would save a lot of time if you confess now.'

'But I didn't kill her,' said Jonathan, eyes wet with unshed tears. Would this detective continue to hound him until he broke down and confessed simply because he couldn't breathe anymore under the weight of the persistent questioning? Was this a tried and tested torture method that had worked before on innocent men?

He glanced at the police officer who sat next to DC Briggs. That man had not asked any questions, but took notes throughout the interrogation.

How much longer would they keep him here? Looking down at his hands he saw they were pale, almost taking on the greyness of the cold stone walls, as if he were slowly disappearing, fading into the surroundings. It had been hours since they'd brought him in for questioning. He dearly wished he had asked to have a solicitor present, but he hadn't thought he would need one; thought there would only be a few questions. How much longer were they allowed to keep him here without charging him? *Surely there must be a time limit.*

His throat felt dry and hunger pangs assailed him, yet with the ever-present nausea he felt sure he would vomit if any food passed his lips.

He began to feel paranoid, lightheaded, and worried he would end up confessing because that was expected of him. As he faced the continual barrage of questions, he wondered if he might be losing his mind.

'How long had you known Mary?'

'I've already told you.' He sighed. 'Two years. We met at a New Year's party two years ago.'

The detective asked the same questions over and over, seemingly on a loop. Would this continue for ever? Perhaps he was stuck in a kind of time warp or a lucid dream.

Jonathan became aware of a closed-in sensation, bordering on claustrophobia. The air felt almost unbreathable—devoid of oxygen. Inhaling deeply, he felt a panic like he could choke on his attempt to breathe. The strip lighting strained his eyes. He wanted to close them, but if he did, he feared he would drift away into a deep sleep; the sleep of the weary and dejected, one in which he would only face nightmares of a different kind.

Right now, he knew he had to concentrate on *this* nightmare. His heart began to beat faster.

Truth be told, he had no idea what happened to Mary. He'd left her at the corner of Haymart Street, where she lived. He'd offered to walk her to her door, but she said she'd be okay. *'I'll be fine, I've had a lovely evening, Jon, thanks for everything. Happy New Year!'* Then that twinkle of a laugh, and she was gone... Those were her last words: '*Happy New Year.'*

'Was she your girlfriend?'

'No, we were just friends.'

'She was seeing a man called Aidan Pearl, we understand. Do you know him?'

'He's her boyfriend.'

'Yet *you* were walking her home?'

'Aidan was out of town. Away on business.'

'So you thought you'd take the opportunity to try to steal Mary away? Were you jealous of their relationship?'

'No. No... It was nothing like that. I've already told you; we were having a New Year drink, that's all. Neither of us wanted to be alone on New Year's Eve. That's all.' He could feel the sweat on his brow, not sure if they believed him, not sure what other "evidence" they were going to present him with.

'You don't have a girlfriend, Mr Graves; is that correct?'

'Yes.'

'Did you find Mary attractive?'

Jonathan fidgeted in his seat, the hard seat that became more uncomfortable by the minute. He didn't like where this line of questioning was going.

The detective's raised eyebrows indicated that he awaited a response.

'She is... *was* an attractive girl.' It didn't feel right, talking about her in the past tense. She had been so alive when he'd last spoken to her; only eight hours before the discovery of her body in the forest, he'd been laughing and joking with her in the pub. Her eyes were sparkling with hope for the new year to come.

They'd shared a kiss at midnight; a long, lingering kiss. Both of them had apologised. 'Sorry,' he'd said. He thought of Aidan; he'd only met him once, but he liked him, and he didn't want to betray his trust.

'No, no. I'm sorry,' she'd said giggling, cheeks flushed. 'I've had a bit too much of this mulled wine, I think.'

'A witness saw you kissing Mary at the bar of the Great Gull pub,' continued the detective.

'It was New Year! We... were only kissing because it's traditional... at midnight.'

'It was more than just a peck, though, wasn't it, Mr Graves?'

Jonathan felt his face grow warm as his cheeks reddened. He sighed deeply and ran a hand through his hair, nervously. 'We'd had a bit too much to drink, got carried away... It was nothing.'

'But you found her attractive,' continued the detective as the other officer scribbled away frenetically in his notepad.

'Look... We are...' He paused for a moment, then said, 'We *were* good friends. We were sharing a drink to celebrate the new year. Where's the crime in that?'

'Mary Bentley was found strangled and sexually assaulted in Bolton Park forest, only a few hours after your New Year's drink. You appear to be the last person who saw her alive.'

Just then there was a knock at the door. DC Briggs began to speak: 'Interview terminated at 9:05 hours.' Switching off the recorder, he stood up.

He walked out of the door, leaving it slightly ajar. Jonathan strained to hear what was happening beyond the door. Whispering and shuffling of paper just out of earshot agitated his anxiety.

The other police officer, the note-taker, stood on the inside of the room observing what was going on outside through the gap in the door; every so often he looked over at Jonathan pensively.

Eventually, the two detectives returned to their seats. DC Briggs no longer had the *we-know-what-you've-done-and-you're-going-down* look on his face. He was now frowning.

'You're free to go, Mr Graves. Thank you for your cooperation.'

Jonathan felt a rush of relief, but at the same time apprehension, as he asked, 'Have... Have you found out who did it? Who killed her?'

'I'm not at liberty to say.'

Two weeks later, the news made the national papers.

Police have been piecing together the last hours of Mary Bentley's life, gathering information from CCTV, witnesses who were at the Great Gull public house celebrating New Year's Eve, and further witnesses who came forward following a police appeal. It is now clear that Aidan Pearl returned home early from a business trip and phoned Mary Bentley's parents to find out where she was celebrating New Year's Eve, telling them he wanted to surprise her. He made his way to the Great Gull pub. The police believe that at the stroke of midnight Pearl witnessed Mary kissing another man; they are working on the assumption that he followed the couple and waited until Mary was alone before he strangled her, after sexually assaulting her. Her body was found in Bolton Park forest. DNA evidence links Pearl to the murder. The pair first met via the Internet on a social networking site, six months before. From speaking to her family, police have discovered that Mary had been unaware of Pearl's criminal record. He served a jail sentence for the attempted murder of his ex-girlfriend, Miss Rose Langton, less than a year before meeting Mary. It is believed Pearl could face a life sentence if found guilty of Miss Bentley's murder. Mary Bentley's funeral took place last week and was attended by close family and friends.

Friends and Neighbours

'Yes, a conservatory would be nice,' said Jill, nodding, 'but they're quite expensive, aren't they?' She sat opposite her neighbour, Rachel, who had come over for a cup of coffee and a chat.

'They're not that expensive these days,' said Rachel, taking a sip of her coffee. She was wearing dark glasses. She always wore dark glasses, even indoors. When they'd first met, she explained that due to a recent infection her eyes were sensitive to light; she'd been advised by an optician to wear the glasses to avoid damaging her eyesight. Jill always felt a little awkward not being able to accurately read Rachel's expression, her eyes obscured as they were by the tinted glass.

'Mine was dead cheap,' continued Rachel. 'As you know, Rob and I have been having financial problems lately, but we still managed to get a conservatory fitted. Where there's a will there's a way, as they say. I always wanted one, you see. Sometimes you've got to throw caution to the wind and do things that you want to do, don't you? No offence, Jill, but you're getting older.'

'Well... yes, I'm a pensioner, dear.'

'You've lived all your life doing the right thing. You should be able to enjoy your retirement. I've heard you talk about how much you love your garden.'

'Yes, Craig and I used to spend hours gardening. I can't do so much on my own... but I still enjoy looking out at the garden.'

'And, how much nicer would it be to do so from the comfort of your own conservatory?' asked the younger woman. 'I love sitting in mine, looking out at the birds and the flowers. We used to live in a house with a much bigger garden, until Rich lost his job—'

'Er... who's Rich?'

'Excuse me?' Rachel flicked her ponytail, and Jill noticed that her cheeks had reddened slightly.

'You said Rich lost his job.'

'No I didn't. I said *Rob*.'

'Oh, sorry, dear, I must have misheard; my hearing's not what it used to be.'

'Yes.' Rachel giggled. 'Or maybe I've got money on the brain. "Who's Rich?" Not me, that's for sure! Wish I was.'

The two women laughed and the tension that had momentarily disturbed the calm began to disperse.

Jill could have sworn the girl said *Rich*, but when she denied it, Jill felt herself tense up. For a brief moment, she doubted her own mind. That happened often lately. Her late husband, Craig, had suffered from dementia and Jill had grown used to looking out for the signs in his behaviour. It frightened her to think of what would happen if she got dementia, especially as she lived alone and would have no one to look after her the way she had looked after Craig.

'Anyway, where was I?' said Rachel. Then, flicking a hand through her ponytail, she continued, 'Oh yeah, I was talking about Rob losing his job, and us having to move here. I told him that if we were going to be living in a terraced house, I wanted to have a garden, and I wanted to be able to sit and enjoy my garden. What's the point of life if you can't do what you enjoy? You should get a conservatory, Jill. If it's what you want, go for it.'

'Hmm... I'm just not sure I have enough money—'

'That's the excuse Rob and I used for not having children. Now I'm nearly forty. We're trying to have a child, but it's harder now I'm older. It will be a burden financially, but we've always wanted a family. We're going to go for it.'

'Yes, children are expensive, especially these days... but it's wonderful that you've decided to start a family. I hope it works out for you.'

'So do I.' Rachel adjusted her glasses. She took another sip of coffee. 'It's always been a dream of mine, just like the conservatory has been a dream of yours. I think you should get one.'

'I have thought about it. Did you say that your husband fitted your conservatory?'

'He did. I'm sure he'd fit yours too, as you're a friend of mine. He's twiddling his thumbs these days, it'll give him something to do while he looks for work. He won't charge you much. I'll have a word.'

'Oh, that's very kind of you, Rachel, but I'll pay the going rate.'

'No. I know I've been moaning about not being able to keep up the mortgage payments, and about not having much money, but you're a friend. We'd do it for free if we could, but there are parts that need to be purchased. You can pay for those. You'll be doing Rob a favour; he hates being out of work with nothing to do.'

Jill looked out of the small window in the back garden door, and began to imagine how wonderful it would be if she could gaze out at the lovely garden to her heart's content from her own conservatory. She couldn't help smiling at the thought. It was as if Rachel had been sent here at the perfect time, when she needed a bit of a lift.

Ever since Rachel and her husband moved in next door, Jill's mood had lightened. Her husband, Craig, had died only six months before and she felt all alone in the world; she'd even been thinking of selling up and going to live with her son, until the young couple arrived. They were like a ray of sunshine. Suddenly it was beginning to feel like home again. 'Let me know how much it'll cost, dear, and I'll decide.'

'Imagine, in a few weeks time we could be sipping our coffee in your new conservatory with a fantastic view of your garden.' The young woman smiled at her, and Jill's heart felt happy.

A couple of weeks later, the conservatory was fitted. 'Don't worry about paying me for the labour, Jill; I'll only charge you for the materials, seeing as you're such a good friend of Rachel's,' said Robert.

'That's very kind of you, but I insist on paying; you've done such a professional job.'

'No, Rach would kill me if I charged you! Let's settle up for the materials, and I'll be on my way.'

After Robert left, Jill shed tears thinking about how lucky she was to have such good neighbours. She had not experienced such kindness for a long time. They were down on their luck, what with Robert losing his job, and then having to move to a smaller house, yet they were so generous with their time. *They really are too good to be true,* she mused. She could feel the anticipation of being able to spend her first evening in the conservatory. Not since she was a young woman had she felt such a rush of excitement. *Rachel was right,* she thought, *What's the point of life if you can't do what you enjoy?*

Jill spent a pleasant evening watching the sunset cast complementary reds, pinks, and purples, across the colourful hues of her flower beds. The conservatory was everything she'd dreamed it would be. Gazing out across the garden, recalling the good times with Craig, she drifted off into a quiet slumber for a while.

When she awoke, her first thought was of how peaceful this little haven was and how extraordinarily kind Rachel and Robert had been; without them, this would have remained an unfulfilled dream. Somehow, she didn't feel worthy of a gift like this from them when she'd only known them for such a brief period of time. Memories of Rachel grumbling about another credit card bill and not being able to keep her finances in the black, filled her mind.

The more she thought about it, it didn't sit well with her that she hadn't paid properly for Robert's hard work, but she suspected Rachel would take offence if she offered money. That thought left a tiny speck of dust on her perfect dream, and she knew she would have to think up a way of paying them back without being too obvious about it.

Casting her mind back to the last time Rachel visited for coffee, she recalled a conversation they'd had about the silver tray that sat on the bench in the kitchen. Rachel had said she thought it was "beautiful". A smile came to Jill's lips. She could give them the tray as a gift. *It must be worth something; it's quite old*, she mused.

Jill glanced at the kitchen clock, and deciding it wasn't too late to visit them, took a plastic carrier bag from one of the kitchen drawers intending to put the tray into it. However, when she walked over to the far side of the kitchen, she stopped in mid-stride and stood stock still. Frowning, she noticed that the silver tray wasn't on the bench where it usually sat.

She began to worry that perhaps her mind was playing tricks on her. This train of thought brought back painful memories.

She almost resigned herself to accepting that perhaps her memory was floundering, but then she remembered Robert had been here for over a week fitting the conservatory... sometimes alone in the house.

She walked into the living room and now saw that her gold, antique carriage clock was missing from the mantelpiece. Looking at the unit, she saw that two of her collectors' plates were also gone. She felt queasy, sure that they were there the last time she'd looked.

Taking a deep breath, she began to check through the cupboards and drawers in the lounge and in the kitchen. To her horror she found that various items were missing: three plates, an antique pocket watch, six silver goblets... The list went on.

Sitting down, she felt torn; part of her wanted to go to the police, but the young couple had financial problems. Perhaps they stole through sheer desperation.

While contemplating this, she heard a dripping sound and realised that it was raining quite heavily outside. Momentarily, a positive thought eclipsed the turmoil in her mind; she felt quite pleased that at least her plants would be watered—it was August and had not rained for a while.

The dripping sound became louder and she heard what sounded like a loud crash. *Was that thunder?* She walked towards the conservatory and saw that half the roof had caved in and the rain was now soaking through the rattan chairs, and cushions.

Jill phoned Rachel's number. No reply. She put on a raincoat and boots, and, grabbing an umbrella, ran next door as fast as her legs would carry her. There was no reply when she knocked on their door: she never saw Rachel or Robert again.

The builder who came to repair the conservatory said, 'It's as flimsy as cardboard, love. How much did you pay for it?'

'Well, I only paid for the materials; a thousand pounds.'

The builder frowned. 'If you bought these materials, you'd get quite a bit of change from a *hundred* pounds.'

The police explained to her that they'd been searching for Rachel and Robert for years now. The couple had a list of aliases as long as her arm. Sometimes they went by the name of Peter and Penny; other times, Jessica and Reg. They changed their names with every move. Their real names were—as far as anyone could be certain—Stacy James and Joseph Peters. They travelled around the country, always using the same scam of building dodgy conservatories and similar structures for vulnerable people, and then robbing them of their possessions.

*

As Jill sat in her son's car behind the removal van, she took one last glance at the house that had been her home for almost thirty years. It didn't feel like home anymore; hadn't felt like home since Rachel and Robert—or was it Stacy and Joseph?—ruined everything; left an indelible black mark on her memories.

She'd put the house up for sale less than a month after the scam. She didn't feel safe living there anymore; couldn't look at the conservatory without recalling how she'd been so easily duped by the fraudsters.

Her son, and a builder friend of his, had fixed the conservatory, but she could only feel a sense of defeat every time she laid eyes on it.

Her heart felt gladdened knowing that the couple who bought the house, Elaine and Jasper, had other plans for the garden.

'Jasper's a bit of a gardener,' Elaine had said when they'd been over to see Jill the week before, after exchanging contracts. 'He's thinking of taking out the conservatory and digging up that area... making a rock pool. It'll look lovely.'

'That will be wonderful,' Jill said, feeling a sense of relief in knowing that the structure would be gone, along with the tainted memory of her deceitful neighbours.

Looking out of the window of the car as they drove away, she mused at how ironic it was that she had been planning to leave this place shortly after Craig died. Her neighbours, the original reason for her staying, were now the reason for her departure.

Jessie looked out of the window to see whether she would need a coat today. The weather was so unpredictable: one day it was hot; the next day it was raining; and the next, she needed a coat, scarf, and gloves.

As she looked down at the street below, she noticed him. Jack. They had been students at the same college, and now here he was, living on the street, destitute. A nobody. He'd been so popular at college. It always helped to put things into perspective whenever she noticed him sitting there. It was almost as if he had been placed there in her life for a reason, to prove that things could be worse. It could so easily have been *her* living on the street.

After being made redundant the year before, she was forced to sell her house to avoid repossession. A memory flickered now, as she looked out of the window; she remembered showing people around her house when the estate agent sent prospective purchasers. One young couple appeared to be quite interested in the property, so she had let them wander around on their own. It was only a small, two bed cottage in a terrace, so she could hear them talking as they walked around. She'd only recently spent three months decorating the house.

'I don't like the wallpaper; it looks so tacky,' said the tall man in a blue pinstripe suit.

His partner replied, 'Well, the whole house needs a bit of a makeover, but it has potential.'

Jessie felt deflated as she watched the couple walk towards her along the hallway.

The woman smiled. 'Er... thanks for letting us have a peek around. It's a nice little cottage. Maybe a bit too small for us. We'll think about it and let the estate agent know.'

'Right, thanks,' said Jessie.

She watched them walk out of the door and along the pathway, and heard the man's voice carry on the breeze: 'Didn't think much of the decor.'

'Yes, but that can be changed,' replied the woman.

'I still think it's too small, anyway,' he said.

Jessie didn't hear any more of their conversation, and in a way, she felt thankful she could no longer hear what they were saying. She felt despondent by that stage: no less than ten prospective buyers had visited in a three month period, but no offers were forthcoming. To add to her anxiety, property prices were falling considerably due to the recession.

She eventually sold the house to a young woman who worked in the local area.

Jessie's total net sale proceeds were £10,000, give or take a few pennies, after paying all her debts and legal fees. She had £10,000, but nowhere to live. Then she'd happened upon this place.

Her parents had sold the shop when they retired, but they kept the flat upstairs. Her father's health was failing due to chronic breathing problems associated with his smoking habit. He ended up bedridden. It proved too difficult for her mother to look after him, so the decision was made to move him to a residential care home. The money needed to pay for the care home ate away at their savings. In desperation, her mother took out a loan.

'What am I going to do, Jess?' asked her mother, sobbing. 'I don't have enough money to pay the loan company and they've sent me a letter... threatening... saying they'll take me to c... court. I don't want to lose my home.'

The tearful call had come as soon as Jessie got home after work, as if her mother had waited by the phone all day, kept an eye on the time, and made sure to call as soon as she got in.

'It'll be okay, Mum; calm down. Tell me more about this loan. When did you take it out?'

'I had a letter a few weeks after your father was taken to the care home. It was offering a low interest loan secured against the property. I thought it would be a good idea...'

'I'll come over tomorrow and we'll sort it out. Don't worry.' Sighing, she put down the phone, wondering how companies could get away with this type of thing. Someone of her mother's age, and in her circumstances, would never be able to pay back a loan.

All of this had happened five years ago, when Jessie was doing well financially. She paid off her parents' debts to avoid the repossession, and the flat was transferred into her name to ensure that no more unscrupulous companies tried to con her mother out of money.

Things went well for a while; her father's health remained steady, and they'd avoided losing the flat. Then her mother began to show signs of dementia. Jessie took for granted that as her mother lived alone, and she didn't see her very often, she could look after herself. Certain recent events told a different story, however.

One day, Jessie had a call from the nursing home.

'Hello, is that Miss Bennett?'

'Speaking.'

'Hello, dear. I'm calling from Open View Residential Care Home.'

Her heart skipped a beat. Why were they calling? Had something happened to her father? She'd only seen him last weekend. She didn't reply, but waited—hardly daring to breathe—for the woman with the soft voice to continue.

'I don't want to worry you, dear, but your mother didn't turn up for her usual visit to see your father today. He was a bit upset, and asked us to call her, but although we've tried a few times there's no reply. It could be something simple, like she forgot the time, or is running late...'

Jessie hardly heard anything after the woman said "forgot"; she knew that her mother had a tendency to forget things lately. Only the other day she'd been to see her in the evening after work and found her watching a boxing match. When she'd walked into the room, her mother was staring fixedly at the screen. Jessie stood silently at the living room door for a moment. She could hardly believe her eyes. 'I didn't know you were a boxing fan,' she said eventually.

Her mother turned to Jessie, eyes wide. Her mouth fell open and then closed, reminiscent of someone trying to mimic a fish. She appeared to be in a sort of trance.

'I didn't know how to change the channel, dear,' she had said by way of an explanation, in a little girl's voice.

'Um... perhaps use the remote control.' Jessie giggled, walked into the room, and pointed to the remote control on the coffee table in front of her mother.

'Sorry, Jess. I'm feeling a bit tired, I think I might just go to bed,' she said, standing up. She walked to her bedroom, entered, and shut the door without saying another word, leaving Jessie to wonder what was wrong.

After ending the phone call with the residential care home, Jessie went to the flat to check on her mother. She had no luck getting through to her on the phone. It kept ringing and ringing. She recalled an incident, the month before, when her mother had left the phone off the hook accidentally, having forgotten to replace the receiver. Jessie went to the flat to check on her then and found she was fine. Her mother laughed it off, saying: 'How the tables have turned. I used to be the one who was frantic with worry when I couldn't get through to you on the phone when you were younger; now you're worried about me. Really, I can take care of myself, love. No need to worry about me so much.'

She did feel worried, though, as she approached the door of the flat. Last time the phone had been off the hook; this time it was actually ringing but her mother wasn't answering. She took a deep breath as she turned her key in the door.

She found her mother lying on the floor, in the hallway. She'd had a fall, she said, and couldn't get up. The place reeked of urine, and her mother seemed confused. After a doctor's visit and a stay at a hospital, it was decided that

41

she should move into the same nursing home as Jessie's father.

The weekly visits to the home were both uplifting and depressing for Jessie. She loved to see her parents, but hated what had happened to them. The cost and responsibility of paying the nursing home fees proved a heavy burden, and soon she found it hard to make ends meet.

The shop owners, old friends of her parents, agreed to buy the flat above the shop from Jessie. That was a relief; now she wouldn't have the upkeep of two properties to deal with.

When she lost her home not too long after that, however, she regretted selling the flat.

By chance, after she sold her own home, she'd been passing by the old shop and noticed the owners had placed a 'To Let' sign there. With the money remaining from the sale of her property, she decided to rent the flat. She was lucky because the shop owners were fond of her parents and felt sorry for her, so they agreed to rent the flat at a reduced rate.

Sometimes she hated living back at the flat with all the memories, but at other times it felt good to be somewhere familiar; somewhere that hadn't changed whilst everything else in her life had been seemingly tossed up in the air in a game played by the gods, and now all that could be done was to wait and see where the pieces would fall.

*

She decided she would probably need a coat, and grabbed it from the coat hook on her way out of the door.

As she exited the building, she saw Jack looking at her. She tried to be polite by smiling at him. She couldn't be sure if he recognised her, so she didn't want to start a conversation with him.

He had an unkempt beard and appeared so scruffy, she worried he might have lost his mind, might be an alcoholic, or on drugs. Who knew what he'd been through in his life to end up this way. She'd often thought of giving him money but wondered if that would make things worse. Would he use it to buy alcohol or drugs? Guilt followed her along the street as she walked away from him. It happened every time she saw him.

Was it was a kind of test? Maybe she should help him. They used to be classmates at college; now here she was, ignoring him, turning her back. *But that was twenty years ago*—she tried to justify it to herself. *People change; he might not be the same man he was back then.* Anyway, she reasoned, they'd never been friends; but she did recall that she had had a crush on him at one time. He'd been good-looking back then. She'd deliberately started talking to him one day at a bus stop outside the college. They happened to be on their way to the same careers fair. She had secretly hoped that if they travelled together to the fair, he would ask her out. He never did.

She had wondered about him, now and then, over the years. Love had not been kind to her and she'd never had a relationship, always falling for men who were not in the least bit interested in her, or who were already taken. Thoughts of those men would often make their way to the forefront of her mind, jolted by a smell, sound, or a sight that triggered a memory. She remembered that she had always hoped to meet Jack again.

When she'd seen him across the road, about a month after she moved back to the flat, his ragged appearance shocked her and brought tears to her eyes. He hadn't changed much underneath the beard and the rough clothing, so it wasn't hard for her to recognise him. She felt a pull towards him then; an almost unconscious pull—a feeling that had never really gone away. But he was homeless. Was it bad that she didn't want to know him now he was destitute? Back in college, she'd have done anything to get his attention. She questioned her morals, and felt uncomfortable seeing him again.

Feeling wary of him, she never did try to approach. He might be violent, of unsound mind.

She rushed past him as she usually did, offering the briefest hint of a smile, not wanting to make eye contact for too long, but not wanting to ignore him completely because that would make her feel even worse about herself.

By the time she reached her office, she'd completely forgotten about Jack, as usual.

Getting Away With It

'So keep your eyes peeled. Those lucky scratchcards will soon be on their way! You could be a winner!'

Scott watched the advertisement with interest. Two hundred scratchcards, in yellow envelopes, would be distributed randomly in one London borough. One lucky prize-winner would be guaranteed to win a million pounds.

He sighed. *If I had a million pounds, I wouldn't have to wake up early every morning to go to work.*

The next morning Scott travelled to the depot and picked up his sack of post. Wearily, he began sorting through the mail and noticed many yellow envelopes. Not quite awake yet, his mind didn't instantly click that these might be the ones with the scratchcards inside. After finding at least twenty yellow envelopes in his sack, he hazily recalled the advert he had seen on TV. Looking around to make sure no one could see him, he carefully opened one of the envelopes. To his delight, he saw there was a scratchcard inside; *It's like Willy Wonka's golden tickets that Charlie was looking for!* Excitement bubbled inside him. Judging by the amount of envelopes in his sack, he'd been given *all* of the two hundred scratchcards to distribute.

He remembered that the man on TV had said the names would be picked by a computer, randomly. It suddenly occurred to him that no one would know if the cards were never delivered!

Temptation taunted him. He would be risking everything, but it could change his life for ever. For the past ten years he'd worked as a postman. Through rain and snow he had delivered the mail. He'd always wished for something better. *But I could end up behind bars. What if someone found out? How could they? Lots of people win the lottery and never claim it. The person who was picked to win this million might never claim it. It's better for it to go to someone who really wants it,* Scott argued with his conscience, yet at the same time tried to justify it to himself.

In this elated state of mind he started to believe that it was more than a coincidence that after seeing the advert on TV the night before, he was now holding the scratchcards in his hands. *It's fate.* He felt like someone who had started reading an engrossing mystery novel; he couldn't stop now or he'd never find out how it ended.

Scott took a diversion from his usual postal route, first going home, where he gathered all the yellow envelopes and hid them under his mattress.

More than one person commented on how happy he seemed to be that morning. Old Mr Jones at number thirty-three Winchmore Street, asked, 'Have you won the lottery, or something?'

Scott handed Mr Jones a brown envelope that most likely contained a bill. He averted his gaze, with a shy smile, avoiding the old man's eyes as a pang of guilt assailed him. *What if Mr Jones was meant to win the million?* But that momentary blip in his buoyant mood soon lifted, and he'd forgotten about poor Mr Jones by the time he closed the gate behind him.

He whistled as he delivered the post, smiled at passersby, and wished a good morning to all the sleepy people who opened their front doors to collect their mail.

His mind dallied in a blissful daze as he thought about what was waiting inside one of those envelopes.

When he got home, he sprinted upstairs to retrieve his bounty. He ogled the envelopes as if they were a delicious meal he could not wait to tuck into. He couldn't help thinking how apt it was that they were coloured yellow—it had always been his favourite colour. The first car he ever owned, a cheap runaround, was yellow. He'd always promised himself he would buy a yellow sports car if he ever came into money. As his smile spread into a grin, he picked up a yellow envelope knowing he was only one step away from a brighter future.

46

Just then, the doorbell rang. Scott's heart began to pound. Had someone found out what he'd done? Frantically, he stuffed all the envelopes back under his mattress.

There was a policeman at the front door. Scott felt lightheaded. *What if they have a warrant to search the place?* His mouth fell open.

'Don't worry, son. No one's died or had an accident,' said the policeman, noticing the colour fading from Scott's face. 'I only want to ask if you know who owns that car across the road.' He pointed to a green car that Scott didn't recognise.

He breathed with relief, although his heart was still beating like a drum. 'Um, no, officer. I'm afraid I don't.'

'Oh, well. Thank you, anyway. Sorry to have bothered you,' said the policeman.

Closing the door, Scott took a deep breath and slowly walked back up the stairs to his bedroom. He began to feel terrible about taking the scratchcards. *What was I thinking?*

He sat on the edge of the bed and unlaced his shoes, kicking them off and feeling the relief after walking all that way on his round.

The police visit had put things into perspective. All he really wanted to do now was deliver the scratchcards to their rightful owners.

As he gathered the yellow envelopes in his hands, however, knowing that each of them contained a piece of card that could potentially alter the course of his life for the better, he couldn't bring himself to let them go. He felt that same excitement that had made him decide to take them in the first place. The proverbial little devil on his shoulder was whispering sweet nothings into his ear.

Before he had time to stop himself, he opened one of the envelopes and took out the shiny, silver card, against his better judgement. A red arrow indicated a small box on the card, inside of which was written, "Scratch here". He found a coin in his pocket and rubbed it on the surface. For some reason, he thought of Alice, in Lewis Carroll's popular tale, and how she had been enticed by the labels, "Eat me" or "Drink me".

Sorry. You have not won the prize. The words mocked him. The remaining envelopes lying on his bedroom floor remained a temptation he could not resist. Shrugging, he picked up another one. *Sorry. You have not won the prize.*

He was now fired up and began opening lots of envelopes and scratching the cards. Soon his fingers began to ache, but he continued to scratch. Then he saw it. The winning card. *Congratulations! You are the million pound winner. Please collect your prize from Cosmos Computer Company at the address below!*

Looking at the address on the envelope, he saw that the real winner was supposed to be Mrs Rose Pendleton. She was a lovely old lady, maybe in her eighties. She always stopped to chat with him when he was on his rounds and she was out for her early morning walk. He knew she had a son who was suffering from a medical condition of some kind. This money could have gone towards his treatment. Scott frowned. He felt like the worst person in the world, as if he had actually gone to Mrs Pendleton's house and stolen her money.

What can I do now, though? I've already scratched it. He made up his mind to collect the winnings and then give a decent sum of money to Mrs Pendleton to ease his conscience. *She doesn't need a million. I'll give her a good few thousand.*

Despite having reservations about what he had done, he couldn't help smiling as he put on his shoes and began to walk to the Tube station. Soon he would be holding a cheque for one million pounds!

When he arrived at the reception of *Cosmos Computer Company*, a young woman looked up from her computer screen and forced a smile as if he had disturbed her: 'Hello, sir. How can I help you?'

'I've come to claim my prize,' said Scott, beaming with excitement. He held out the scratchcard.

The receptionist took the card from him and stood up to shake his hand. 'Congratulations, sir.' She smiled, and even fluttered her eyelashes at him.

Scott realised that, being a millionaire, he would now be more attractive to the opposite sex. Pretty young women, like this receptionist, usually made him feel invisible.

'I'll just go and get the boss; he'll be able to verify your claim.' She walked away, but swivelled round briefly to smile at him again.

Hmm, maybe I'll take her out for a drink later, he thought, returning her smile.

She disappeared into the back office.

Scott took a seat in the reception area and began to dream about what he would do with the money.

Shortly, the "boss" arrived; a tall man, at least six foot, with a sleeked back hairstyle, and a wide smile. 'Good morning, sir. I'm Edwin Granger—manager of Cosmos Computer Company—pleased to meet you; and may I extend my hearty congratulations to you!' he said, shaking Scott's hand. 'Can I have your name, so that I can write out the cheque?'

'Of course. Scott Coombs.'

Scott smiled, but began to feel self-conscious. What if the cards had not been distributed randomly? And what if the company knew the identity of the person who was supposed to win the money? Sweat formed on his brow.

'Thank you,' said Mr Granger, handing Scott a form. 'I need you to complete this for security purposes.' He began to write out the cheque.

Scott could not believe his luck. It was all so easy. He filled in his details on the form—name, address, occupation—and handed it back.

'Thank you, sir. I've already written out your cheque.'

Scott's eyes greedily took in the small slip of paper held between the manager's forefinger and thumb. That tiny bit of paper would be life-changing. As Scott's smile grew wider, images of tranquility danced through his mind: exotic beaches, piña coladas, and the receptionist scantily clad in a bikini, rubbing sun cream onto his back...

Impulsively, he looked over the front desk at the young receptionist.

She winked at him.

Blushing slightly, he smiled then turned away, recalling the image of her that had been in his head only seconds before.

'I'll just check this,' continued the manager, interrupting Scott's dreams.

Edwin Granger scanned the form and then looked up at Scott, his once smiling mouth now downturned. He lowered the cheque out of Scott's reach.

Scott's heart began to beat faster as his hand shot forward in a desperate attempt to somehow stop the cheque, and his promised land, getting away.

'Sorry, sir. I'm going to have to invalidate your claim, unfortunately.' He was now holding the cheque behind his back, wary of Scott's outstretched arm.

Scott bowed his head, let his arm fall to his side, and envisaged handcuffs, police cells, and a prison uniform.

'I see you're a postman,' continued Mr Granger, pursing his lips.

Scott nodded. He knew theft from an employer was an imprisonable offence; he'd read it somewhere. He began to shake involuntarily.

'The scratchcard clearly states that employees of Royal Mail cannot claim the prize. I'm so sorry, sir.' Mr Granger shook his head and appeared truly sympathetic.

Scott breathed a sigh of relief as he watched him walk away and disappear into his office. 'Phew! That was close!' he said out loud.

The receptionist narrowed her eyes at him, puzzled by his reaction, then went back to typing something into her computer, just as she had been doing when he'd first walked in.

He loitered for a while at the front desk, wondering whether he would still be in with a chance of taking the receptionist out for a drink. She didn't look at him, kept her attention firmly on the screen in front of her.

He faked a cough.

She turned towards him. 'Can I help you, sir?' she asked, quite sternly.

'I wondered if you'd like to go out with me sometime.' Even to him that sounded lame, and he was inwardly squirming.

She glared at him, then said, 'I already have a boyfriend, sorry.' She looked back at her computer screen.

When he said good-bye, she appeared agitated. The smile she had worn earlier was a distant memory, replaced by something that resembled a grimace. 'Good-bye,' she said glumly, without even looking in his direction.

Scott shrugged and walked away.

'Batty old woman; I told her a sob story about how you lost your job and needed something to do with your time,' said Stacy, rolling her eyes.

'Huh! That's the problem with people today. They think you have to be working in a crummy nine-to-five job to be happy. You and me, babe, we've worked it out,' said Joe, running a hand through his thick blond hair.

'Yeah.' Stacy smiled and sat on his lap, shaking back her ponytail. 'That old bat has probably got thousands of pounds worth of antiques in her house; you can easily take 'em. She won't notice, she's as scatty as they come.'

'Perfect!' he said, leaning back in his chair.

Stacy laughed and kissed him on the mouth. 'I'm so glad I met you!'

'Okay,' he said, pushing her off him. 'Haven't got time for this lovey dovey stuff. I've got a job to do.' Then he frowned. 'Y'know, there's a flaw in our plan.'

Stacy rubbed the side of her hip, which had collided with the edge of the table when he pushed her away. 'What's that?' she asked, screwing up her forehead and trying not to appear too offended that he'd rejected her advances.

'The flaw is,' he said, standing up and crossing his arms in front of him, 'fitting these conservatories, porches, *et cetera*, is too much like fucking hard work.' With a mock sigh, he walked past her.

'Are you sure we won't get caught doing this?' she asked.

He turned around to face her. 'Of course not. I'm a pro; been doing this kind of thing for years before you came along. I've always been able to get away with it. I've got the gift.' He grinned widely, displaying perfect white teeth.

She wished he would pay her more attention. The only reason she'd agreed to get involved in this get-rich-quick scheme was because she had fallen head over heels for his model looks. She felt foolish whenever he treated her like a spare part.

Recently she could feel them drifting apart slowly. She was trying to stop that happening, but he was becoming more distant. He always seemed to be plotting the next "job". She suspected he might be having an affair, but she wasn't ready to face up to such a reality, so never confronted him about it. What would happen to her if he left? It frightened her to think about that. For almost two years, all she'd done was follow him around. She felt a dependency that she often resented.

*

Stacy and Joe met through a mutual friend a couple of years before. Since that time, they had moved around the country putting Joe's money-making plan into action. When they'd first met, he'd lived in a nice home—more of a mansion—in the countryside. He bought it from the proceeds of a "nice little bank job" that one of his friends, Tony, had done.

He'd given up his job as a builder when Tony gave him the money for the house purchase. It turned out, however, that Tony only needed him to launder the money; moreover, Tony had taken the lion's share of the cash when there were other gang members who had played a bigger part in the heist.

Joe received threats from several of the gang members. When one of them threatened to kill Stacy if he didn't hand over the cash, Joe promised he would sell the house and give them the money. He managed to stall them for a while saying that the house sale was taking longer than expected.

Eventually, he sold the country house and bought a smaller one out of town with the cash Tony said he could keep for helping him launder the money. He'd given the balance to Tony, knowing full well that the other gang members would be irate about that.

Joe thought up the conservatory scam, partly from the need to stay on the run, for fear of the gang catching up with him; and partly as a way to make enough money to live on. Over the years, he had pilfered bits and pieces from many construction sites while working as a builder, and knew he could put the materials to good use, fitting conservatories and similar structures.

His heart wasn't really in it, but the money was good, especially with the extras that he could steal from his clients' homes.

He felt obliged to bring Stacy along with him for the ride, because her life had been threatened by the gang. If he'd gone missing on his own, they might have got to Stacy somehow, and as much as she was starting to annoy him at the time, he couldn't live with that on his conscience.

These days, everything she did grated on his nerves. He rued the day he met her. In hindsight, he knew that the only reason he'd started seeing her was because he happened to be going through a dry patch where women were concerned, and she had practically thrown herself at him. Desperation, he now realised, was never a good reason to get into a relationship.

He acknowledged that he could be partly to blame for Stacy's apparent obsession with him, as he'd given the impression he liked her at the beginning. It was fun for a while, but even the sex was boring now. About two months ago, he'd started seeing Rhonda, from the local supermarket.

When he'd first met Rhonda, she was serving behind the counter; there were hardly any customers in the shop. He walked up to her and noticed the wedding and engagement rings on her left hand. *Bingo!* he thought. Married women were always the easiest to bag, and a challenge at the same time. They always liked to pretend they gave a damn about their vows, so he enjoyed playing the game. He found that the ones who protested the most were the ones who would give in to his advances the quickest. Of course, it helped that he had inherited good looks from his father. People often commented that he resembled a young Robert Redford. Joe had to Google that name as he'd never heard of him. It was true, though, he did bear a striking resemblance to the actor.

When he approached Rhonda, and said, 'What's a stunner like you doing working in a place like this?', her cheeks turned a deep crimson. That was the thing about married women; mostly, they didn't have much experience with men apart from their own husbands. They were easy to please.

'I'm a married woman,' she had said, giggling and batting her eyelashes at him: a green light signal, as far as he was concerned. They went out to a pub that night. Her husband wanted to watch the football on TV, and she wasn't interested. It didn't take long for Joe to persuade her out of her knickers.

The great thing about Rhonda was that she didn't demand a relationship from him. He merely represented a temporary release from the stagnation of her married life.

Stacy, in comparison, screamed for attention. Much too needy. He could hardly bring himself to sleep with her anymore. Most days he tried to think of the best way to leave her. He often found himself regretting not leaving her when he'd fled from the gang. In his darkest moments, he caught himself trying to work out a way to contact the gang anonymously so he could inform them of Stacy's whereabouts.

He had to admit, though, Stacy had a way of convincing the old people to part with their cash. They made a good team; that's why he'd put up with her for so long. They pretended they were married, and changed their names all the time. At the moment, they were Rob and Rachel. He had a hard time remembering the pseudonyms.

Lately, he noticed Stacy appeared to be getting increasingly caught up in the lie; as though she believed it to be true that they were a couple. This bothered him.

Joe didn't want a relationship; women bored him. Whenever he wanted sex he would go to a local bar or club and pick up a woman too drunk to know any better, and go back to her place; or he'd find a married woman like Rhonda to fulfill his needs. Married women were notorious for their liaisons; he'd read somewhere that thousands of married men—as many as one in five—were unaware they were bringing up other men's children. Joe didn't want to get tied down like that. He only slept with Stacy when he was desperate.

Once in a while he felt guilty about leading her on and bolstering her delusion that they were a couple. But he didn't have time to think about that.

Often, he wanted to cut and run; drop her, and carry on doing the jobs on his own. However, she had a bit of a crazy streak, could be so erratic; he couldn't trust her not to grass on him if he dumped her and shattered her illusions.

Far from being the free life he had imagined for himself, more often than not he felt trapped.

He dreamt of making enough money to pay her off, but was sure she thought they had a future together. Short of killing her, he didn't know how he would ever be rid of her.

When she sat on his lap and kissed him that day, it was like the straw that broke the camel's back. She was so deluded. He decided he would have to end it.

Remembering he had half a dozen concrete slabs from an old patio job he once did on an extension, he knew he could easily hide the evidence. The problem was twofold: first, he had to kill her, and second he had to somehow get her dead body into the old woman's house next door, so he could hide the remains beneath the new conservatory.

In the end, it turned out to be much simpler than he had expected. A whack to the head with a frying pan was all it took to kill Stacy. Quick and effective. He hardly felt any remorse.

Old Jill, next door, said she would leave the door on the latch for him in the morning as she was going shopping. The universe had ostensibly conspired to assist him with his plan.

Digging the ditch in the back garden proved to be the hardest part, and it was stressful as he kept looking at the door, worried the old woman might return before he managed to bury the body. He didn't want to have to kill her too. He knew he was a deft hand with a frying pan, but wasn't sure that he would get away with both murders.

His one-way ticket out of the country had been booked. The only thing left to do was bury Stacy, then he could make his escape.

Later that day, he felt pleased when Jill commented on how lovely it was to have paving slabs on the floor of the conservatory. 'I wasn't expecting that,' she'd said, smiling.

Stacy wasn't expecting it either, Joe mused, scaring himself at how chuffed he was that things had gone so smoothly.

That evening, on board flight 3389 to somewhere he couldn't even pronounce, Joe imagined the old woman sitting in her new conservatory, sipping tea, unaware that Stacy was lying underneath the paving slabs. His frown turned into a smile when he noticed the air hostess with long wavy hair giving him the eye. His own eyes strayed down to the ring finger on her left hand. *Bingo!*

Seeing is Believing

'Sooz! What happened?' Katie reached out towards her friend who was standing outside the front door, cheeks wet with fresh tears.

'S..S..Sorry to... bother you so late... in the evening,' said Susan through sobs. 'Is it... sorry, is it all right if... if I come in?'

'Yes, yes of course.' Katie stood aside to let her through into the hallway. 'What's wrong?'

'I've... I've left Nick.' Susan went into the living room and continued to cry uncontrollably.

'Why?' Katie reached for the tissue box and sat next to her friend.

'He's been... he's having an affair.'

'Oh, I'm so sorry.' Katie handed her a tissue, while thinking *Bastard. I knew he'd do something like that!* She remembered telling Susan, when she'd first met Nick, that there was something she didn't trust about him.

'It's okay,' continued Susan, 'y... you don't have to... to pretend,' said Susan through sniffles, 'I'm surprised you're not say... saying "I told you so". I know you've ne... never liked him. You've always said he... he was wrong for me. Looks like you were right all along. Why didn't I listen to you? You know, my... my sister said the same thing. I never listened to her, either.' She wiped her eyes as she spoke. 'I... I thought he lov... loved me.'

Katie stood up. 'What's love, anyway?' she said. 'I don't think many people know what it means anymore.' She sighed, her mind now recalling memories of a brief affair she'd had with a man she met online. Antony. They'd dated for a few months. She fell head over heels for him—even found herself flicking through wedding magazines looking for dresses, and thinking up names for their future children. Antony told her he loved her, but had been seeing three other women at the same time. Looking back, she wondered how she could have been so deluded. She shook her head, as though trying to rid it of the unwelcome thoughts that brought back feelings of betrayal and remorse. 'I'll make us a cup of tea,' she said, disappearing into the kitchen where she could shed a few tears without Susan seeing her. The pain was still raw.

'Can I stay here tonight?' asked Susan, when Katie returned with the tea.

'Yes. You can stay as long as you like.'

*

Susan was still asleep on the sofa when Katie left for work the next day. At lunchtime she decided to go home to check on her.

As Katie stood at the traffic lights in the high street waiting to cross the road, she saw Nick in the distance with a tall, brown-haired girl. *That must be the girl he's been having the affair with*, she thought, shaking her head.

Nick put an arm around the girl and kissed her cheek. They appeared to be waiting at the bus stop.

How come he gets to be happy when Sooz is so sad, thought Katie, glumly, giving the couple the evil eye, even though they were facing the other way and wouldn't have been able to see her.

When she got home, she found a note on the kitchen table.

Katie, thanks for letting me stay last night. Nick phoned me this morning and we had a chat and sorted things out. He said the affair was only a one-night stand and he regrets it. I've decided to give him one last chance. I know you probably think it's the wrong decision, and maybe I'm being a fool, but I love him. Don't worry about me. I'm happy. Thanks again for your help last night, I really appreciate it. See you soon, love Sooz x

Katie could hardly believe what she was reading. *He's brainwashed her!* Grabbing her mobile out of her handbag, she dialled Susan's mobile. 'Hi Sooz, it's me.'

'Katie? What's wrong? You sound out of breath.'

'Nick is *still* having an affair. I saw him on the high street, about five minutes ago, with another girl at a bus stop. They were kissing.'

'Wh... What?'

'Sorry. But I just couldn't let you go back to him knowing that he's lying to you.'

'Do you think they're still at the bus stop?' asked Susan after a brief pause.

'Probably... yes. Look, if you don't believe me, meet me there in five minutes. Can you get there?'

'Yeah, okay, which one is it?' said Susan, sounding jaded.

Katie gave her the directions to the bus stop.

As Katie approached the high street, she could see Nick in the distance with the girl. A satisfied smirk contorted her features; finally he would pay for lying to Susan for so long. She crossed the road and was now very close to them.

A window cleaner was on a ladder to her left, cleaning a shop window, and Katie noticed a bucket of water on the ground.

Nick and his bit on the side were only a few feet away at the bus stop, arm in arm. They had their backs to her. Katie's eyes were drawn again to the bucket of water. The temptation was too much to resist. Picking up the bucket without giving herself time to change her mind, she threw the soapy water all over them, then stood back, grinning.

Her mobile phone rang, so she quickly put the bucket down, wiped her hands on her skirt, and fished the phone out of her bag, still smiling. 'Hello?'

'Hi Katie, it's me.'

'Sooz!' Her smile grew wider as she watched the couple who were now soaking wet. She couldn't wait to tell Susan about it.

'Listen, you must have made a mistake about seeing Nick at the bus stop. I just called him at work. He's there.'

'But—' Katie was about to protest when she saw that the couple had turned towards her. She shuddered as she noticed that the man had the same hairstyle, wore the same type of clothes, and was the same height as Nick, but he *wasn't* Nick.

The window cleaner had now come down from the ladder and was holding the bucket frowning.

Nick's double was rubbing the soap suds from his eyes. He glared at the window cleaner and began shaking his fists at him: 'You idiot! Look what you've done!'

Katie turned around and began walking away as fast as her legs would carry her.

Delusion and Dreams - Part III

Frances pushed the buggy along the high street wondering how she'd ever ended up like this; a mother of six children. She knew she should be grateful that at least she was financially able to stay at home and look after them. *How do working mums cope?* It baffled her. The day-to-day routine was a never-ending list of things to do. Marc helped as much as he could, but he was a man who had no idea about child-care related issues, and Frances didn't have the patience to teach him.

She had been at a low ebb personally, lacking in self-esteem, when Marc came into her life.

Growing up, she had always worn NHS glasses for her shortsightedness, as her parents couldn't afford the cost of a decent pair. She was ridiculed throughout her school years for wearing the monstrosities, especially when the plastic frame broke and her mother stuck it together with a brightly coloured sticky-tape. As the sticky-tape was pink, her mother assumed she'd be thrilled with it. The tape turned out to be luminous.

One afternoon, in a chemistry lesson, the teacher dimmed the lights to present an experiment to the class. Laughter emanated from the back of the room and slowly spread as the pupils noticed that Frances's glasses were glowing pink where they'd been secured with tape. That incident earned her the nickname "glow-in-the-dark speccy-monster". To make matters worse, around that time Frances developed a bad case of acne.

In the summer break before they were about to start college, her best friend Nina suggested she get a perm as they were fashionable at the time. Frances had always had straight hair and was very self-conscious about her new perm, which Nina admitted perhaps didn't really suit her. Frances's hair had been shoulder length, but the perm made it shrink to just below her ears. No one told her that her hair would appear shorter after the perm. If she'd known, she would never have agreed to it. Nina's sister, a hairdressing trainee at the time, said she'd do the perm for free. The result was a frizzy mop on top of Frances's head. Denise—the hairdresser—assured her that it would look great when the hair grew a bit. It never did look "great".

For the next few months, Frances lived with a disastrous perm that was taking forever to grow out. Whispers and laughter behind her back brought back memories of her awkward youth when she had spent an inordinate amount of time alone and hiding from people who might pick on her because of the way she looked.

Frances preferred to keep her hair on the longer side, because she thought her square face was a bit too masculine-looking. The result of the perm at the age of sixteen for a girl who was already lacking self-confidence was to create a withdrawn and moody teenager.

Her misery was compounded when, that year, as a gift for successfully passing her exams, her parents bought a new pair of glasses that they said they had saved up for all year. 'You're always complaining that you have to wear those NHS ones,' said her mother, beaming with delight. 'We wanted you to have a nice pair now that you're growing up. We chose them, specially. They're from a designer range.'

Her father watched on, a wide grin on his face, as Frances tore open the green and gold wrapping paper.

The first thing she noticed when she saw the glasses was that they were enormous. Almost like goggles.

'Try them on, darling,' coaxed her father. 'The woman who served us at the shop said these are the most popular ones on the market. Lots of celebrities wear them, you know.'

Frances removed her NHS glasses and put on the new gold-rimmed ones.

'Beautiful!' exclaimed her mother.

Frances stood up and went over to the mirror above the fireplace. She almost threw up when she saw her reflection. Holding in the outburst that she knew would upset her parents, she ran out of the room before any tears had the chance to fall.

For the next few months, until she managed to save up a bit of money from her Saturday job to buy a new pair, Frances felt obliged to wear the glasses; not only because her parents had spent so much money on them, but because she couldn't see a thing without them; and as embarrassing as the new ones were, she didn't want to go back to wearing the old NHS pair.

Her teenage years were difficult to get through. To add insult to injury, almost all the clothes she wore as a child were hand-me-downs from her older sister, who had inherited them after they'd been worn to death by their eldest sister.

While wheeling the pram along the high street, she wondered for the fiftieth time that morning how she had ended up like this. She'd always sworn never to have children, or maybe only to have one or two if her partner *absolutely* wanted them. After growing up with five siblings, she told herself she should have known better. Times were hard for them growing up.

She knew she didn't have to worry; Marc had a great job—they were doing well. That was not what really bothered her, though. As a young girl she'd had dreams; wanted to make something of her life, not end up a housewife with lots of children and a husband who was hardly ever there, and more precisely was just someone she lived with. The romance was long gone from their relationship. Sometimes she wondered if she'd ever really loved Marc. He came into her life at a time when she needed someone to make her feel desirable. She'd been young when they got together, and had still believed in happy endings.

At college, a turning point for her—one that reawakened the feelings of isolation and ostracism from her younger years

—was when a boy named Jack made fun of her in front of the whole class of about twenty students. 'Here comes Deirdre Barlow,' he'd said as she walked into the economics lesson one day.

She'd waited for a humourous quip, or for him to say: 'Only joking.' It didn't happen.

Looking around the room briefly, she hoped someone would say something to defend her; but all she saw were faces trying (mostly unsuccessfully) to stifle laughter and giggles.

Even Nina was laughing. Frances knew she looked a sight with that perm and those glasses, but she'd never expected this. She sat at her desk, focussing on the board at the front of the room, trying to ignore the whispers and giggles, hoping the teacher would arrive soon to distract the attention from her.

'Oy, Deirdre,' said Jack. 'How's Ken these days?'

She didn't turn to face him.

'Leave her alone,' said his friend, Phil, also laughing.

'It's true though, isn't it?' said Jack. 'She looks just like her, with that hair.'

'It'll grow,' said Nina, giggling. 'It'll be so much better in a week or two.'

Frances's face felt hot and tears threatened to fall, but Jack and the others prattled on, oblivious to her pain. *Why can't they change the subject?*

'She'll still have those glasses though, won't she?' said a voice she couldn't place, but she didn't want to turn around to see who it was. She wanted it all to stop.

'And that blouse,' added Jack, with a snigger. 'I'm sure Deirdre was wearing that on *Corrie* the other week.'

'Okay, enough,' said Nina, now serious.

Frances had by now stood up and was walking out of the room.

Jack apologised to her later, saying it was only a bit of a joke and he thought she would find it funny because he'd heard her laughing about how the perm had gone wrong, and had even heard her refer to her glasses as "Deirdre

65

glasses" in the past. She accepted his apology, but felt self-conscious for months afterwards.

As soon as she left college, she went to work at the local fast food restaurant, whilst seeking a "proper" job. That's where she met Marc. He was only twenty-five, but already the manager of the restaurant. They had a fling because he was the first man who had shown interest in her in that way. She got pregnant, they got married, and the rest was history.

Now, in her mid-thirties, she had a house full of children. After having the eldest, Eleanor, the couple planned another child, hoping for a boy. They had another girl, Joanna.

The girls were aged sixteen and fourteen now, and typical teenagers. Frances's head was always full of concern. Would they make friends with the wrong people, or get into drugs and alcohol? They were such sweet girls, frequently she worried they'd be taken advantage of, or be bullied like she was.

A few years after Joanna was born, Marc got it into his head again that he wanted to try for a boy, to "complete" their family. They did try, but the result was twin girls. Sophie and Jess were aged seven now.

A couple of years ago, Marc once more suggested that they try for a boy, saying it might be their last chance as they were getting older. So last year, she'd given birth to another set of twin girls, Kim and Rebecca. She gave serious thought to getting herself sterilised in case Marc suggested they try for a boy again.

She felt worn out with all the running around after the children. Whenever she complained, Marc would say she had it easy as she'd never had to go out and work for a living. He made her feel guilty saying she didn't appreciate how hard he worked to provide her with a luxury lifestyle. He now owned a chain of restaurants. It was a multi-million pound business.

The thing was, Frances felt envious when she met career women; their lives always seemed so much more exciting than hers. At the age of nearly thirty-seven, she wondered whether the chance of a career had passed her by. Marc never listened when she tried to talk about maybe doing a distance-learning course to brush up on skills and qualifications. He kept saying there were millions of women who would kill to be in her shoes. She sighed, aware that from the outside her life looked good; but that was the thing about thoughts, wasn't it? No one could see them. Often she was screaming inside.

These days, Frances only went to the best hairdressers. She always ironed her hair, and wore contact lenses instead of glasses. For herself and the children, only designer clothes would do. Nothing less. Yes, on the outside, all appeared perfect. Her inner turmoil remained an invisible burden she kept from people she met. Even from her closest friends. Not that she had any close friends. Most of them were acquaintances, at best; other mothers she'd met at her children's schools. There was Shirley—a girl she used to know at college—but Frances always made an excuse every time she invited her to meet up. She couldn't get over the fact that Shirley had known her back then; back when she was that girl everyone used to make fun of. It felt like there was a brick wall she couldn't get past. Whenever Shirley phoned her, or popped over to the house for a chat, Frances seized up, became a different person. Perhaps, she mused, that was why she'd drifted away from all her high school and college friends—even Nina, her best friend. Without having to see them, she could choose to forget the difficult years, reinvent herself without judgement, and try to mend her heart.

The thoughtless throwaway comments of that one boy twenty years ago, left a scar in her psyche, deeper than an ocean, it seemed. People had no idea of the power their words could hold.

She cursed out loud as one of her stiletto heels got stuck in a grate. Parking the pram, she bent down to assess the damage. The shoes were brand new and had cost £300. She sighed when she noticed a scratch on the heel, and wondered whether she could take the shoes back to the shop and exchange them for another pair; she racked her brain trying to remember where she'd put the receipt.

Peering over the pram, she was pleased to see that the twins were asleep. A quick glance at her watch told her there were two hours to kill until she had to collect Sophie and Jess from school.

As she was about to take the brakes off the pram and walk away, her eyes were drawn to what she'd thought was a pile of old rubbish, near a wall on her right, but it had moved. It was a person. He turned his face towards her. *Jack?* she thought. His beard was thick, but those eyes were a dead giveaway. She'd fallen in love with the colour of his eyes.

'Jack... It is you, isn't it?'

The blank expression on his face told her he didn't recognise her.

'You must be mistaken,' he mumbled, but his voice confirmed his identity.

Reaching out a hand, she offered to shake his. 'You don't remember me, do you?' She smiled sweetly. 'Frances.'

'I would shake your hand, but I haven't washed in days; don't want to spread any germs.' He pointed at the babies in the pram. 'Frances?' he queried, shaking his head to indicate that the name hadn't meant anything to him.

'Yes... Frankie. From Southgate College. Picture me with a perm and the round glasses. Deirdre Barlow, remember?' She found herself laughing.

'Oh...' His mouth fell open. 'Sorry.' He placed a hand over his face.

'Water under the bridge,' she said. 'Can I buy you a coffee?'

Merry-go-round

Mandy wiped the perspiration from her brow. She stood by the cooker in the steamy kitchen preparing the family dinner. Eight-year-old James was running around chasing Scooby, the dog, and pulling his tail. Meanwhile two-year-old Emma was constantly pushing the button on her "Dora" doll, which kept singing an annoying repetitive song, and whenever Mandy tried to take the doll away, Emma would start crying. From the living room, music of untold decibels, threatened to shatter all the windows (well, that is if it could be called "music"), as eleven-year-old Peter attempted to play his electric guitar.

Mandy was at her wits' end, feeling sure she must have repeated herself at least a hundred times: 'Stop pulling Scooby's tail, James; stop pushing that button, Emma; Peter, turn that music down! I've got a headache!'

Her husband Dave had returned home from work but immediately disappeared upstairs to have a shower, not offering to help with the children—as usual.

This was the daily routine. Some days Mandy felt like she was on a merry-go-round of sorts, where—after much to-do—she would always end up in the same place: back where she started, feeling dizzy and confused, but knowing she'd have to do it all again *ad infinitum*.

When she did finally manage to gather the family around the kitchen table for dinner that evening, the food was already getting cold, and James and Peter ended up having an argument, which resulted in most of their food ending up on their clothes. Mandy's next task was to try to get the children washed and ready for bed, against their will. It was a never-ending repetitive cycle and she knew it would start again in the morning at seven o'clock when she had to wake up the children and get them ready for school on time.

The next day, after settling Emma down for a midday nap, Mandy went into the kitchen for her "luxury" hour, when she would sip a cup of tea whilst listening to her favourite radio station playing soft melodic tunes, or read the latest romance novel. She put her feet up, and, through sheer exhaustion, fell into a deep sleep.

When she opened her eyes, the first thing she noticed was the kitchen clock: *six o'clock*. 'Oh my God!' she said out loud. *The children have been home for ages,* her mind whirred; *and Dave will be home any minute. I haven't even started cooking dinner yet!* She rushed over to the fridge to take out the food, but then stopped, sensing something was wrong: it was far too quiet for it to be six o'clock: Peter's music wasn't blaring from the front room, and James wasn't running around making a nuisance of himself and annoying the dog. Miraculously, Scooby was sleeping quite peacefully in his bed in the corner of the kitchen. This didn't seem right. *Where is everyone?*

She walked through the hallway and into the living room, where—to her surprise—she found Dave, James, and Peter, sitting around the table. They were all smiling.

Perhaps my real family were abducted by aliens and replaced with these people... She couldn't help smiling back at them. 'Hello, what are you doing?' she asked, feeling strangely nervous, as if this was some kind of set-up.

'We're playing *Monopoly*,' said Dave, brightly.

'*Monopoly*?' Mandy's eyes widened.

'Yes, it's a board game, where you go around the board buying property,' said Dave.

'Oh, ha, ha, very funny... but—'

'When the boys got home from school they saw you were sleeping,' explained Dave, 'so they didn't want to wake you. They decided to come in here and play some games. I thought I'd join them.'

I wish I'd known that all I had to do to get a bit of peace and quiet was to fall asleep! 'Oh, that's nice,' she said, her eyebrows raised in disbelief. 'I'll just go and make dinner.'

'No, love, that's okay,' said Dave. 'I've ordered a pizza. I thought we'd give you the night off.'

Mandy looked at James and then at Peter, bemused: they had actually been sitting there for more than five minutes without arguing with each other. She was tempted to pinch herself; feeling sure her eyes were deceiving her. *Where's my camera?* she wondered, wanting to take a picture of this moment and frame it so she could remember this feeling when times got tough.

'Mum, come and join us,' said Peter. 'We've only just started playing.'

'Um... I'll go and make sure Emma's okay first.'

'There's no need, love,' said Dave. 'My sister, Alice, has taken her for the evening. She says she'd like to baby-sit more often.'

'Oh?' said Mandy whilst thinking: *This all seems to good to be true.*

She dearly hoped it would be the start of a new era, as she took a seat next to them at the table.

'You have to choose which one you want to be,' said James. 'I'm the hat, Dad's the ship, and Pete's the car.'

They were like a proper family at last. *Maybe the boys are growing up?* Her heart filled with pride as a smile spread across her lips. 'Okay, I'll be the dog.' Picking up the little silver dog, she placed it on the game board.

'Mum, you can't be the dog!' James's brow wrinkled into a frown. 'Scooby is the dog.'

'Scooby can't play *Monopoly*,' said Mandy, giggling.

'No, it's true, Mum. It's Scooby!'

She sighed and turned towards her son as he began to shout: 'It's Scooby, Scooby, Scooby!'

'Stop shouting, James!' she said, feeling deflated, realising that the perfect family picture was shattered and things could only go from bad to worse.

Peter then stood up and switched on his amplifier: 'I'm going to play some guitar,' he said.

'No!' she screamed.

Then she woke up to find James running around the kitchen, chasing Scooby and pulling his tail. The amplifier was turned up to full volume in the living room, so the screeching guitar drowned out the sound of the smooth melodies she had been listening to on her radio. Another noise joined the commotion, as Emma's cries sounded from the baby monitor.

Courage

James was afraid of many things: birds, planes, clouds, dogs, the moon, and the dark. He had been nicknamed "Yellow chicken" by a bully at junior school and the label stuck. He couldn't really argue against it either, when he was prone to jumping involuntarily whenever a plane flew overhead or a bird landed next to him or flew onto a nearby tree. He always crossed the road when he saw a dog approaching, even if it was with its owner, on a lead, and wearing a muzzle. He never looked at the sky if he could help it; too scared to see all those clouds moving about. And the moon—well, it was too imposing; so white and big against a dark sky. James also suffered from claustrophobia and at the same time agoraphobia: he just couldn't win.

When he first started secondary school and no one really knew him, he tried his best to fit in and to hide his phobias. A few weeks into the first term, two of the older boys approached James and his new friend, Greg, after school at the bus stop.

'Are you first years?' asked the taller of the two boys. He had a scruffy head of black hair, and large blue eyes that appeared to be popping out of his head.

'Yes,' said Greg.

'Well, we'd like to welcome you to the school,' the boy said, smiling at his friend, a stocky boy with brown hair and glasses. 'Are you settling in all right?'

'Yes, thanks,' said James and Greg in unison.

James had been a bit worried that the boys were going to pick on them, but he now felt more at ease.

'What're your names?' asked the black-haired boy.

'I'm James.'

'Greg.'

'I'm Paul and this is Wes,' he said.

'Nice to meet you,' said Greg, extending a hand to shake Paul's, but Paul ignored the gesture. Greg withdrew his hand, his face turning slightly red.

'You may not be aware of the initiation challenge that we set first year boys,' said Paul.

'Initiation? What's that?' asked James, finding his voice.

'It's like a way of introducing you to the school, but also making sure that you are loyal and can be trusted to carry on our good name when we leave. We're in our last year and we want to find a couple of boys to replace us. We're leaders, if you like.'

'You mean like prefects?' asked Greg.

'Hmm, not quite,' said Paul.

Wes laughed at the comment.

'What are you responsible for then?' asked James, seeing that Greg's cheeks had reddened again.

'We're part of an elite group. A secret society, if you like. We're well respected. Other schools used to cause a lot of trouble for the pupils of Delamere High before we came along. Gangs from other schools used to beat up the first years and steal their lunch money. Then we came along and stopped all that. This is our territory, and the local gangs know that. There's respect for that. We're the ringleaders now; they're scared to try anything. We're revered. Infamous, if you like.'

'But I thought you said you were a secret society,' cut in Greg. 'How do the other schools know about you?' He frowned.

'Has he swallowed too many text books, or something?' Paul directed the question to James, who instinctively lowered his eyes to avoid Paul's stare.

'Are you a smart arse or somethin'?' Paul asked Greg.

'N... No... I just wondered—'

'Huh! Too much thinking will rot your brain.' Paul snarled at Greg. 'Look, the less you ask about us, the better, okay? We'll tell you all you need to know in good time. The main thing is, there are gangs around here that will prey on our first years if we don't protect them. Yes, we expect a bit of respect in return. Is that too much to ask?' He looked from Greg to James and back again. 'Well?'

Both boys shrugged.

'Good,' continued Paul. 'Now that you know the basics, we'll explain what you have to do.'

'So, you're not chosen by the teachers then?' asked James.

Paul glared at him, as if he had said something stupid.

Wes laughed.

'Let's just say we're a group of independent students,' said Paul, a hint of aggression in his voice.

'What sort of things do you do?' asked Greg.

Paul twisted to face him and shook his head. 'Are you always so annoying?' Then directing the question to James, 'Is he always this bloody annoying?'

Wes laughed, and both James and Greg glanced at him and then each other with furrowed brows. All Wes seemed to do was stand and laugh, from time to time eyeing each of them in turn with a mocking stare. His silence was chilling.

The number 22 bus appeared at the end of the road.

'That's our bus, Greg,' said James, sighing openly with relief.

'Ah, well, it looks like we'll have to explain things to you tomorrow then,' said Paul. 'Meet us here after school and don't be late. And tell your parents that you'll be late home.'

'Late?' Greg's voice came out quite high pitched.

'Yes, it may take time to explain all the rules, you see.'

'Do we have to come?' asked James, who had noticed Greg's creased brow, and how he was fidgeting nervously. James hated bullies, having put up with enough of them at junior school because of his phobias. 'Can't you find other boys to intimi... I mean, initiate?'

'No,' said Paul, gruffly. 'Make sure you're here tomorrow, or we'll have to assume you're traitors, and then things might get a bit tough for you at this school.'

'Are you in a gang?' asked Greg, small grey eyes wide open, so the whites could be seen around them.

'Stop asking so many questions, you freak. Just be here tomorrow,' said Paul, leaning over so that his nose almost touched Greg's, a threatening scowl on his face.

Wes began laughing again.

James shivered.

Once on the bus, Greg turned to James, biting a fingernail as he spoke: 'Do you think we should tell a teacher about those boys?'

'I don't know,' said James. 'If they find out, they might beat us up. It sounded like there are more of them; maybe a gang.'

'I know.' Greg was now visibly shaking with nerves.

'Don't worry though, Greg, I've dealt with bullies before; you have to stand up to them.' He recalled being pelted with eggs as he was leaving his junior school one day, and then covered in flour; the other time, when a boy had threatened him with a knife in the playground and forced him to smoke a cigarette; and the time when he'd been forced by a bully to break another boy's glasses. He'd never stood up to bullies before, so he didn't know how he would do it now. The more he thought about it, the more he began to feel nauseated.

'I think I'm going to tell a teacher,' said Greg. 'They must be able to do something.'

'I just think things might get worse if we tell a teacher. We have to meet them. Besides, there are always lots of people at the bus stop, so they can't do anything to us there.'

'But what if they ask us to go somewhere with them?' Greg had turned a ghostly shade of pale.

'We won't go.'

'Aren't you scared?' asked Greg, tears threatening to fall.

'Scared? Me? No,' said James. He had fought all his life to rid himself of his phobias, and the one thing he'd heard over and over from people was that you should "face your fears". He decided it was time for him to do just that, no matter how frightened he felt.

The following day, after school, James and Greg got to the bus stop to find that Paul and Wes were already there.

'So you came, then?' said Paul. 'I thought you two would bottle it. This shows we were right to pick you to join our mission. You've got guts.'

James started to feel a bit better, but noticed a confused frown on Greg's face.

'Come with us,' said Wes. The first words they'd heard him speak.

They followed the older boys, who walked past the bus stop and along the street.

'Right,' said Paul, when they were a fair way from the bus stop. 'Your task is simple. It's a game called "Chicken". You may have heard of it?'

James and Greg looked at him blankly. James started to feel paranoid, worried that they had somehow heard about his old nickname.

'You can go first, smart arse,' said Paul, pointing to Greg.

James turned towards his friend and saw him physically quake.

'Wh... What do I have t... to do?' he stammered.

'The buses stop at that bus stop there, right?' said Paul.

The boys nodded.

'Right, well, what you have to do is wait until the bus has started off again and wait for it to build up a bit of speed; which it will by the time it gets here. Then jump in front of it and back again, really quickly. The thing is, though, you have to cause the bus driver to brake, otherwise you've failed. And if you fail, we'll have to punish you.'

'Wh... What sort of punishment?' asked James, seeing the colour drain from Greg's face.

'Something like making you eat something nasty, or steal something, or maybe flushing your head down the loo. We'll think of something.' Paul smiled, grimly.

Wes laughed.

'I'm not doing it,' said Greg, walking back towards the bus stop. 'Come on, James; they're bullies.'

James couldn't move, his mind full of painful memories of what he'd suffered at the hands of the bullies at his other school.

'Greg, if you don't do it, then your friend will have to do it twice and if he fails even once, we'll punish *you*.'

Greg stopped walking. 'James, aren't you going to stand up to them?'

Stand up to them. Stand up to them. The repeated advice James had heard throughout his life, as if he was somehow to blame for the continued abuse.

'Right, the bus is coming,' said Wes, grabbing James's arm. 'You have to jump in front of it, remember?' His face flushed with excitement.

James took a deep breath. *How hard can it be?* he wondered, *to dodge a bus?* Surely he could do it and then these boys would be off his back; they might even become friends and then he'd never have to worry about bullies ever again. *Face your fears.* The words drifted into his mind again.

'Okay, I'll do it,' he said loudly.

'James, no!' shouted Greg.

Wes was still holding James's arm.

The bus's front indicator light began to flash, showing that it would be setting off from the bus stop. Wes pushed James towards the kerb.

As the bus gained momentum, James felt Wes grab his arm tightly and try to move him into the road. Without thinking, James turned towards Wes and pulled him over his head, like a sack of potatoes, even though Wes was twice his size.

Paul's eyes widened, and Greg's mouth fell open as they watched from the side of the road.

Wes crashed to the ground after doing a somersault in the air, landing right in front of the bus. His glasses fell onto the road after he did, and they skidded towards where Paul and Wes were standing, ending up on top of a drain.

The driver put his foot on the brake and the bus mounted the kerb. The front of the vehicle collided with a lamp post, sending many of the passengers flying, so that they ended up with cuts and bruises.

Wes had to be taken to A&E. Paul disappeared from the scene before the ambulance and police arrived. James and Greg later found out that the older boys got in trouble with the police the year before when they forced a first year pupil to play the "Chicken" game, and the boy was injured and almost died.

Greg and James gave statements to the police.

James was asked to accompany the police to the station for an interview.

*

'That was a reckless act. People could have been killed in that accident,' the policeman said, frowning, as they sat in the interview room.

James shivered as he contemplated what could have happened. The way he felt now paled in comparison to how he had felt when faced with any of his phobias. He remembered Wes grabbing his arm and then all he could remember was seeing the boy lying on the ground in front of the bus.

'I'm s... sorry... I don't know what happened. It was self-defence... he was going to push me in front of the bus.'

The two policemen who sat across from him looked at each other and then at James's dad who'd been called to sit in with him for the interview.

'James is a good boy,' said his dad, sweat on his brow. 'He was bullied in primary school so we sent him for self-defence lessons. If you ask me, they came in handy. It could have been my son under that bus.'

Tension filled the room.

'You're a very lucky young man that I'm not arresting you,' said DC Roberts.

The older boys' reputations seemed to be an influence in the police decision to be more lenient with James.

Eventually, they allowed him to go home.

At school the next day, James felt like a local hero. Some of the children who had been bullied by Paul and Wes, told him their stories and seemed in awe of him. Many of them said he was brave to have stood up to the older boys. For the first time in his life, James was popular. He felt elated, almost as if he was walking on air.

As Greg and James walked towards the bus stop that afternoon on their way home, an irrational fear gripped James. The sensation of being afraid felt all too familiar, but the object causing his fear was different.

'I... I think I'm going to walk home,' he said to Greg.

'But, it's over a mile. It's much quicker to get the bus.'

'No...no... I'll see you tomorrow,' said James, running along the street, too afraid to look over his shoulder in case he caught sight of that big, red, frightening... bus.

Delusion and Dreams - Part IV

Frankie told me she would talk to her husband about getting me a job in one of his restaurants.

'Marc owns lots of restaurants,' she said as she sat opposite me in the little café. She'd bought me a doughnut and a coffee. She was sipping on a green tea. Said she was watching her figure; but there's not a hint of fat on her. If I didn't know better I'd say she was anorexic.

Frankie was wearing a really strong perfume, and I had to hold my breath a couple of times when she leaned towards me. I wondered whether her two children were really asleep or if they'd been knocked out by the fumes. She's changed a lot since we were at college. She seemed... I don't know... *different*, somehow. I suppose we're older, and life may not have been all she'd hoped it would be, but it's like she's trying to be someone she's not. There's nothing of the old Frankie left. Even her voice sounded different, like she's faking her whole self.

She doesn't wear glasses anymore; that's one of the reasons I didn't recognise her in the street. When her buggy stopped in front of me and I saw this lady in expensive clothes, I expected her to give me a bit of loose change. Some people do that; makes them feel less guilty about their privileged lives, I suppose. Most people ignore me, though. Maybe acknowledging me would be like admitting something is wrong with their perfect world.

Frankie wears contact lenses now. I only know that because she accidentally dropped one of them in the café as she was leaning over to check on the twins. She searched for it frantically. 'I always get paranoid that I'll drop one of these things and one of the kids will swallow it,' she said. She had a spare pair of contacts, and asked me to watch her twins while she went into the toilets to replace the one she'd lost. That spoke volumes to me; letting a homeless man you had only just met again after twenty years, look after your babies. Either she was hoping I would kidnap them (she was moaning to me a minute before about how hard it is to cope with four young children, and two teenagers), or she was more concerned about her appearance than her kids. I'd guess the latter.

That was about three months ago. I'm not sure if she came back here looking for me and didn't find me. Maybe she has been looking for me, but I'm usually here. I haven't seen her since the day she bought me coffee. She gave me two hundred pounds—said that was all she could get out of the cash machine. 'I'll come back and help you,' she said when we parted. 'No one should have to live on the street, in this day and age.' Those were her exact words. I'm still living on the street.

Not that I'm complaining. Sometimes I think I'm one of the lucky ones. I watch people going to work, coming home from work. Like robots. I don't have to do anything. I don't even own a watch. If I did, it would probably be stolen while I was asleep, anyway. It's tough out here. You always have to watch your back. It's most dangerous at night. I try to stay hidden as much as I can at night.

I've found a place I can go for free food, and a public place I can go to have a wash. I'm finally one of the *real* homeless people of London, I guess. A young man from a homeless charity visits me a few times a month; he wants to help me get back on my feet, he says.

I often wonder why Frankie didn't return. Maybe her husband wasn't too keen on helping a homeless man. Maybe he warned her off me. I guess I'll never know. I still wait for her to come back every day. Sad, isn't it?

I don't really want to hang around this area much longer, my reason for staying here is over. Jessie has a boyfriend. I think they're getting married. I saw a ring on her finger last week; that was the last time I saw her. She spends less and less time in her flat. She's always out and about somewhere... with him, probably. Don't get me wrong, I'm happy for her. She deserves to be happy. She smiles more now. Seems content. She doesn't notice me anymore. I have become invisible to her. She used to smile at me, albeit sympathetically; now she simply passes me by.

Part of me wants to hang around here waiting for Frankie, but I can't bear to see Jessie with that man. Dan is his name. I heard her calling him from the door when he was leaving one day. They often stand outside the door chatting before he leaves. They always kiss. Sometimes I imagine that it's me she wants and she's only trying to make me jealous. I know what you're thinking: it's ridiculous; I'm deluded. Yes, maybe I am. But you haven't had to walk my path. I have come to learn that sometimes it's only our dreams that keep us alive.

Bonus stories:

Flames

She's pretty, thought Robert, looking at the girl who had just sat next to him on the park bench. *Looks a bit like a young Cindy Crawford.* She had originally sat quite close to him, but was now shuffling along to the other end of the bench. Blushing, Robert realised that he'd been staring. Averting his eyes, he pretended to read the novel he held in his hand, whilst thinking what a beautiful shade of green her eyes were and how her emerald earrings complemented them.

When he felt brave enough to look at her again, he saw that she was sitting at the far edge of the bench, almost sideways, as if to avoid his gaze. He couldn't blame her, after all it was a big city; for all she knew, he could be a mass murderer. Then, he became concerned that perhaps she'd moved away from him because he was suffering from a body odour problem that no one had told him about. *I'm sure I used my antiperspirant this morning.* As much as he wanted to have a sniff of his armpits, just to check, he felt too self conscious. Shrugging, he carried on eating his sandwich.

Robert had just started working for a new company and hadn't been out in this part of town before, so he was now secretly hoping that this girl would be someone he'd see every day. *Perhaps she works close by. Maybe we'll bump into each other every lunchtime and become friends, and then...* He was getting carried away with his dreams as he stared blankly at his novel whilst finishing off his sandwich. He stole a glance at her again, from the corner of his eye, and noticed that she was fiddling with one of her earrings. *What should I say?* he thought, desperate to talk to her; but he couldn't think of anything to initiate a conversation. *And anyway*, he reasoned, *she probably wouldn't want to talk to me, judging by the way she's moved to the other end of the bench.*

Feeling the need to look at her again, but not wanting to make it obvious, Robert twisted around to face her and held up his book in front of him. Now, he was able to watch her from behind the pages. *I wonder what her name is? She must have a beautiful name, something to suit her face... Elizabeth, perhaps, or Angela... No, something unusual like... Eloise, or... Amelia.* Her perfume fragranced the air around him, a floral, feminine scent, that captivated his senses.

When she'd finished her sandwich, she reached into her handbag. As she did so, their eyes met, snapping Robert out of his daydream. He saw that his book was now on his lap, and realised that he'd been staring at her again. Looking at his watch—a universal embarrassment cover-up —he felt the colour rise in his cheeks. She'd smiled at him, and he was finding it hard to meet her eyes.

He took a deep breath, and once he'd recovered his composure, he saw that the girl was facing away from him. *How am I supposed to talk to her now?* he thought. The small window of opportunity that had been offered to him was now closed. It seemed so unfair. Back at square one, he could do nothing but stare at her long brown hair falling in soft curls over the back of her cream-coloured blouse. The sun caught the golden highlights in her hair and he imagined running his fingers through it. Aware he was almost gawping, he withdrew his gaze and watched people rushing through the park, noticing it was very noisy. In wonder, he recollected that while he'd been staring at the mysterious girl who sat beside him, he'd hardly known that there was anything else going on around them.

Just then, her mobile phone sounded, rousing him from his awestruck thoughts. She didn't have a silly ring tone on her phone, Robert noticed, just a traditional ringing sound. Then he remembered his own *Star Trek* ring-tone and, feeling embarrassed, prayed his phone wouldn't ring. He thought about switching it off.

'Hi,' she said, and for a moment he dared to dream that she was talking to him, but when he turned towards her, he saw her holding the phone to her ear. She appeared more relaxed as she spoke on the phone, and leaned back on the bench, so now he was able to see one side of her face. *Oh, what a perfect profile*, he thought. *Like an angel.*

She laughed, and an unwelcome thought struck Robert: perhaps she was talking to her boyfriend, or husband. An irrational jealousy took over his mind. He had never believed in love at first sight, and had laughed at his sister just the other night when she'd told him how much she'd enjoyed the movie, *While You Were Sleeping.* He remembered telling her, in no uncertain terms, that if she believed all those romantic comedies she watched, she would end up very lonely and disappointed. His feelings were now completely alien to him.

The girl on the bench laughed and flicked her hair back from her face, then continued speaking on the phone. He couldn't make out what she was saying, and longed to be able to hear her voice without the sounds of traffic, other people's voices, and general city noise that was drowning it out. Tempted to move closer to her on the bench, he thought better of it; she already seemed a bit nervous of him.

In a few minutes, she stood up, brushing off a bread crumb from her pink skirt, and picking up her handbag. Her eyes met his briefly and he wondered whether she also felt something; an unexplained connection. But then she walked away, disappearing into the crowd, gone as quickly as she had arrived.

Robert watched her leave, unable to stop her, wanting to follow her. He looked at the bench where she'd been sitting—an empty space. *Why didn't I say something to her?* Her perfume still lingered in the air around him. He breathed in deeply and recalled how she'd smiled at him. Regret tugged at his heart.

Looking back at the far edge of the bench, his soul screaming for her to reappear for an instant so he could talk to her, he noticed something small and shiny where she'd been sitting. It glimmered in the sunlight as he moved closer. His mouth fell open in wonder when he saw it was one of her emerald earrings that so matched her eyes. He reached to pick it up, excitement coursing through his being; now, he would have an excuse to talk to her. Gathering his belongings from the bench, he began to walk briskly in the direction she had headed. *She'll be easy to spot,* he thought, *long brown hair, pink skirt—she can't have got very far.*

He moved quickly through the lunchtime crowd, bumping into a couple of people along the way. After a few minutes he came to a crossroads and stopped walking. It became clear that he would not catch up with her. She'd probably turned a corner somewhere. Sighing, he realised the futility of his search among the hordes of city dwellers going about their busy lives like swarms of bees.

Robert returned to the bench at lunchtime the next day, and the next, and the day after that, always taking the earring with him; hopeful. *She will return*, he told himself. She never did.

The earring became a symbol of this woman, a kind of charm that he carried around with him everywhere. When he looked at it, he remembered her face, the golden highlights in her hair, her perfume, the green of her eyes, the way her skirt hugged her hips, the sound of her laugh, and the way she had smiled at him.

Two years later, Robert lost the earring. He used to carry it around in his wallet. One day, as he was taking out a ten pound note, the earring slipped out onto the ground, unseen by Robert. He was at a music festival with a girl he had been dating for a few months. They were queuing at a food stall. The ground was soggy from rain, a mush of grass and soil. The earring made no sound as it fell. Robert and his girlfriend, Sally, walked away from the food stall carrying their fish and chips. Sally stepped on the earring with her wellington boot, lodging it firmly into the ground; following her were other festival goers, so the earring became completely buried in the soil.

Later that evening, Robert was about to place his wallet under his pillow for safekeeping.

'How much cash do we have left?' asked Sally.

'Um.' Robert opened the wallet and began to finger through the notes, 'Ten, twenty—' then he stopped, his mouth wide open.

'What's wrong?' Sally looked at him. Even in the half darkness of the tent, she could see his face had fallen; he appeared distraught. 'Have we been robbed?'

'I've lost—' He stopped, thinking better of it. How could he say "I've lost an earring"? It would sound absurd. Then he had a flash of inspiration: 'I've lost an earring that my nan gave me on her deathbed. I used to carry it with me everywhere; it reminded me of her.' The words 'reminded me of her' resounded in his head as he recalled long brown hair falling in curls down the back of the girl of his dreams, as she walked away from him two years before.

'An earring?' Sally screwed up her face. 'Why only one? They come in pairs. It seems odd. Was your nan only wearing one earring?' Sally smiled as she lifted her bottle of beer to her mouth to take a sip. Then, noticing that Robert didn't return her smile, she said: 'Sorry, I didn't mean to sound insensitive... It's just, well, I have this image now of your nan only wearing one earring.' She stifled a giggle.

Robert was in no mood for jokes. He felt numb. He had lost his one remaining connection to the girl who had stolen his heart. Until this moment, he never realised how much the earring meant to him. It had been a way of keeping the door open for his soul mate to return to his life, a way of keeping the flame alive.

Without thinking about it, he stood up. 'I'm going to look for it,' he said, gruffly.

'But... it's dark. Anyway, how do you know you lost it here? When did you last see it?' Sally frowned.

'This morning,' he replied. 'It was in my wallet this morning.'

'It's too dark to look for it now, wait until tomorrow and I'll help you look for it,' said Sally.

'I've got a torch,' he said.

Robert spent two hours retracing his steps around the park, shining the torch on the ground, all the while knowing his search was in vain; but he had to try. To give up would be like letting go. He felt like a fool when he thought of the many broken relationships he'd had in the past couple of years all because none of the girls he dated could make him feel the way he'd felt about the girl on the bench. It was like a curse that followed him everywhere, and he could do nothing about it.

At 3 a.m. he gave up and returned to the tent. Sally was asleep. He made up his mind that he would tell her it wasn't working out between them. It wouldn't be fair on her now that he knew he still had feelings for someone else. He'd be leading her on, knowing that he could never care about her in the same way.

The next morning, Sally nudged him: 'Wake up, Rob, we're going to miss that band you wanted to see.'

His head felt groggy. 'What time is it?'

'Late enough. I've overslept because those girls in the next tent didn't shut up until after two o'clock. I'm sure they were drunk. They were talking so loud. I'm going to get breakfast, coming?'

'I'll follow,' he said, fully intending to leave the festival and make his way home before Sally got back. He knew it was cowardly, but he couldn't tell her face to face that he was leaving her. He resolved to send her a text message.

*   *   *

Anne woke up in the tent next door to Robert and Sally. Stretching, she looked over at her friend Susie, who was still asleep. Anne thought of Steve, as she often did each

89

morning. If she hadn't broken up with Steve, they would have been together at this music festival, but they split two weeks ago. Susie had persuaded her to come to the festival, saying she'd accompany her: *'It'd be a shame to waste the tickets, and it'll do you good to get out and forget about him, instead of moping around the house,'* she'd said. Anne wasn't so sure. Being here brought back memories of the year before, when she'd been at the festival with Steve.

Sitting up and wriggling out of her sleeping bag, she reached into her handbag and took out her compact mirror. Running her fingers through her dyed black hair, she found herself wondering whether Steve would like it. She shook the thought from her mind, reminding herself that he didn't matter anymore. A frown creased her brow.

Susie had convinced her to dye her hair and try a new hairstyle, saying that a change would help her forget Steve. Anne had lived with him for over a year before finding out that he'd been seeing another girl for at least three months. She found a few text messages on his mobile and confronted him about them; he'd walked out the door without saying a word, never looking back, not apologising —leaving her to heal her own wounds and wonder why.

Anne was still unsure about her new hair colour— whether it suited her or not. Her hair had always been light-brown, and in her 25 years she'd never dyed it. And she'd always worn her hair long, but now it only reached her shoulders. Shrugging, she put the compact mirror back in her handbag and changed into her jeans and T-shirt. She picked up her bag and sunglasses. Susie somehow slept through all of this. Anne didn't have the heart to wake her; they'd been up chatting until after 2 a.m.

Stepping out of the tent, she knew what she wanted to do. She wanted a portion of chips for breakfast. Last year, she and Steve had shared a portion of chips for breakfast. She still missed him, and found herself wishing he was with her. As a tear threatened to fall from her eye, she put on her sunglasses. A young man walked out of the next tent, she nodded and smiled at him.

'Hello,' he said. He looked a bit grumpy, annoyed about something. His face was familiar, but she couldn't place it. Perhaps she'd seen him yesterday when they were setting up their tents. She walked past him quickly before he could say anything else, because his demeanour was quite intimidating, and she felt worried that maybe she and Susie had kept him awake last night when they were laughing and chatting.

Walking towards the food stalls, she could see a few people milling about, but it was early and none of the bands had started playing, so it was quiet. As she approached a van which had "*Fish and Chips*" emblazoned in green lettering across the top, she hung her head, feeling a bit glum as she again remembered being here with Steve the year before. Something shiny caught her eye, sticking out from the mud next to the van. *Perhaps it's a pound coin?* Wondering if she'd be lucky enough to get a free breakfast, she bent down and picked it up, cleaning off the dirt. She was amazed to see, in her hand, an earring, exactly like the one she'd lost two years ago.

Steve had given her the pair of emerald earrings after their first date and she'd worn them every day. Gold drop earrings with beautiful green stones, which Steve said matched her eyes. Having a habit of fiddling with her earrings, she often found that she was missing one. Usually she would find it again, somewhere in her house, but she'd lost the emerald earring one lunchtime in a park. After lunch, she'd returned to the office where she worked, and Kelly—her colleague—had asked her why she was only wearing one earring. Anne had rushed back to the park, retracing her footsteps all along the street and through the park, but she never found the earring.

As she looked at the shiny piece of jewellery in her hand, she wanted to believe that it was the same one she had lost. It wasn't one of a kind; there were probably thousands of girls who owned the same pair, but she couldn't help thinking that it was a sign. She'd been thinking of Steve when she found it.

Anne took a tissue out of her handbag and cleaned the remaining mud off the earring, wishing she'd kept the other one, but she remembered throwing it out not so long ago. As she placed the earring in her purse, she resolved to keep it with her always. It was like a connection to Steve, something to hold onto, to keep the flame alive. *Maybe one day we'll get back together.*

*   *   *

Robert walked out of his tent and saw a young girl with very dark, shoulder-length hair, wearing sunglasses standing outside the next-door tent. He remembered Sally complaining that the two girls in that tent had been talking loudly well into the early hours.

The girl looked at him, nodded and smiled. He said 'Hello', to be polite, but his mind was still in shreds about how best to end it with Sally. He was in no mood for small talk with a stranger, and hoped this girl would not try to speak to him. Frowning, he tried his best to look unapproachable.

As the girl with the dark hair walked past him, he caught a breeze carrying a fresh, floral perfume, that brought with it memories of a warm summer day somewhere back in time, but he couldn't remember quite where he had smelt that scent before.

Robert walked away in the opposite direction and took out his mobile phone to text Sally. **I'm going home. Don't try to contact me. It's over. It's not you, it's me. Sorry. Bye.**

After sending the text message, he wondered whether he'd been too blunt. Shrugging, he made his way out of the park, thoughts of the girl on the bench still haunting his mind.

Isolation

'I don't know what we're paying that psychiatrist for.' Amy's mother's voice was laced with anger.

'I want to stay at home with Becca today,' said Amy.

Her mother frowned. 'You spend too much time on your own, it's not good for you. Your father has taken time off work today. We told you we'd be going out to dinner for your birthday.'

Amy averted her eyes from her mother's steely gaze. Sometimes she felt like a caged bird; spending more and more time in isolation in her bedroom. Whenever her parents came to see her it was to ask if she was "all right", or to suggest a family day out. Dr Grube, the silver-haired psychiatrist, had recommended that they spend more time together as a family unit because many of Amy's issues sprung from her being an only child and not spending enough quality time with her parents.

For the past six months, Amy had been having weekly counselling sessions. She knew she didn't have any "issues" and that her parents were wasting money on this doctor who could do with a bit of analysing herself, judging by the multicoloured psychedelic dresses she wore.

Amy's one sanctuary from the overprotection was her best friend, Becca. If it wasn't for Becca's visits, she felt sure she'd have been driven insane by her parents and their overanxious ways that stemmed from their own guilt.

After her mother left the room, Amy looked at Becca apologetically. 'Sorry about that. My mum can be rude at times. My parents are so concerned about my well-being that they often forget how to treat me or my friends well.' She laughed dryly.

Becca twirled a lock of brown hair around her fingers. 'Let's go to the park. It's a nice day; the weatherman said it would hit 30 degrees.'

'Okay,' said Amy, feeling odd, realising that this would be the first time she and Becca had gone outside together.

Becca usually visited her at home and they stayed in her room to chat and play. Amy's mother constantly told her that it was dangerous for young girls to play outside; she warned of monsters lurking around corners, or in the back of cars and vans, waiting to devour passing children. Perhaps the visits to Dr Grube were paying off, because when Becca suggested going outside, Amy had not broken out in a cold sweat.

Taking a deep breath, Amy walked towards her bedroom door, feeling a sense of freedom; as though she were breaking out from a cocoon of fear. The furthest she had ventured outdoors lately, was to her parents' car for her trips to see Dr Grube.

Amy was home-schooled. Her parents didn't want to send her to the local school. They said she would meet the wrong people and pick up bad habits. When she complained that she wouldn't make any friends if she stayed at home, her parents bought her a dog. Jinx was a cute and energetic puppy. Amy was happy to have him, and for a while her feelings of loneliness were forgotten. Her parents would only let her play with the puppy in the back garden.

One morning, when he was just two years old, Amy found Jinx shivering in his kennel. He appeared unwell. Her father took him to the vet and returned empty handed. Jinx was suffering from pneumonia and the vet wanted to keep him in the surgery under observation. A phone call the next day confirmed that the puppy had died. Amy was inconsolable. She blamed her parents for not letting Jinx sleep indoors. The snow had been covering Jinx's kennel for over a week before he fell ill.

She locked herself in her bedroom and then the pattern began, where she would spend most of her time alone. Around that time, Becca came into her life. Becca didn't think she was crazy, in fact, she'd once told her she thought her parents were the crazy ones. She was thankful for Becca; a lifeline to her sanity.

Amy went into the kitchen, where her mother sat at the table reading a novel.

'Mum, I'm going out.'

A gasp from her mother relayed her shock and surprise at the news.

Amy turned away towards the front door and began walking briskly.

'Wait! Amy!'

Amy stopped walking, but continued to stare at the front door as if it were an escape route, longing to reach it before the invisible but powerful reigns could stop her. 'Me and Becca are going out,' she said, resolutely, to the door.

'But, you're not well, honey.' Her mother was beside her now, holding her shoulder. Her voice sounded patronising to Amy who longed to break free from her mother's strangulating hold.

Amy looked at Becca who smiled back at her. This gave her the courage to reply: 'I'm going out. It's my birthday and I'm going to spend it with my friend.'

'But your father and I—'

'I want to be with Becca today.' Her eyes were now brimming with tears.

Her mother rubbed her back and said, 'Becca can come with us. There'll be chocolate cake.'

'I'm not a child!' came Amy's sharp response.

'You're only twelve years old, Amy, of course you're a child,' said her mother, gently, one hand remaining on her back.

Amy shrugged free and looked at her friend who stood twiddling her hair. Why wasn't Becca standing up for her? It had been Becca's idea that they go to the park. 'Why aren't you saying anything?' Amy stared accusingly at her friend.

Becca turned away.

'What do you want me to say, honey?' asked her mother.

'I wasn't talking to you!' said Amy, a tear escaping from her eye.

'Calm down. Your father will be back from work soon and we'll go to dinner.'

Amy looked daggers at her mother, and when she turned back she saw that Becca had already left. Regret coursed through her veins; she wished she hadn't snapped at her. It wasn't Becca's fault. Her heart hollow, she worried that Becca might not want to be her friend anymore.

Amy began to cry, and soon felt surprised to find that she was not swimming in an ocean of her own tears. Where did all the tears go when they fell? They were gone; seemingly dissolved on the way from her eyes to her cheeks. Some had slipped into her mouth. She knew because of the salty taste they left behind. Her mother was cradling her; rocking her. When Amy lifted herself up, she saw that her mother's shirt was wet; stained with tears. A reminder of the pain.

She stood up, unable to look into her mother's eyes.

'Darling, stay here with me for a while. Let's talk,' her mother said, seeming reluctant to let go of her arm.

'I'm going upstairs,' she replied. As she said it, a blackness enshrouded her. She didn't want to go back up there, to that room where she was always alone. She wanted to run free, to get away. So, she did. Darting out of the front door, as if a starter pistol had sounded, she ran and ran, and she kept on running. A feeling of liberation took over and brought peace to her troubled mind. She heard her mother's screams behind her, fading. Soon, they were too distant to be heard.

Amy woke up in hospital. She had collapsed after running for quite some time, and was almost run over by a car. There had been much whispering between the doctors and her parents before they let her go home. Frustration overwhelmed her: *Why won't anyone tell me anything? I'm not a child!*

Her mother looked at her as if she had run out of words. Neither of her parents spoke to her in the car. The silence was absolute.

When they arrived home, her father said, 'Amy, we don't know what to do for the best. Dr Grube will be coming to see you this week. She'll know what to do.' Doubt flickered in his eyes.

A few days later, Amy was in her bedroom when there was a knock at the door. She hoped it was Becca. She hadn't seen her since the evening of the accident.

Dr Grube opened the door and entered the bedroom as if she had been there a hundred times before, when in reality she had never visited Amy at home. Amy didn't like the way Dr Grube was looking around the room, as if she were searching for signs that a mentally disturbed individual inhabited this place. Before she even sat down, Dr Grube took out her pen and jotted something down in her notebook, which seemed to be glued to her hand, because Amy had never seen her without it.

The doctor smiled briefly at her and then sat on the pink armchair in the corner of the room. 'Hello, Amy. How do you feel today?'

'Fine,' she replied. The good old word that could be used in place of all and any other true feelings. She found herself wishing hard that Becca would turn up, so that she wouldn't have to be here alone.

'I understand it was your birthday last week,' said Dr Grube. Leaning over, she reached into her briefcase pulling out a red parcel tied with a bright pink bow. She stood up, walked towards the bed, and handed it to Amy along with an envelope. 'Happy birthday!' she said, brightly.

Amy took the gift and card, unsure how to react. She had not expected to receive anything from the doctor. Their relationship had always been very distant, stifled, and uncomfortable. Dr Grube had hardly shown any real human emotions in all the time she'd known her, and Amy always resented the way she tried to delve into the deepest reaches of her mind. 'Thank you,' she managed to say eventually, almost under her breath.

Dr Grube returned to the pink armchair and sat down. 'Now, Amy,' she began, 'tell me how you are feeling.'

Amy's eyes were drawn to the birthday present. She wanted to know what was inside, but it appeared that the doctor had now reverted to formal mode. Her face was full of concern, reminding Amy that this was not a social visit.

Amy cleared her throat. 'Um... I'm fine.'

'Let's talk about the day of your birthday. Why did you run away? Are you able to tell me?'

Amy recalled the claustrophobia that had enveloped her and the way she had sensed a freedom as she escaped the confines of the house. She met up with Becca at the end of the road, and they played a game. They ran along the street, trying to stay on the narrow kerb, running in a straight line. The road was busy, and as it became darker they used the lights of the passing cars as a guide. She remembered Becca running ahead of her, laughing at her because she could not keep up.

'Amy? Are you okay?'

Dr Grube's voice roused her from her memories; it was as if she had been lost back in time.

'I'm fine,' said Amy again.

'Tell me about when you ran away. Where did you go?'

'I was with Becca.'

'Oh.' Dr Grube frowned and made another note in her little book. 'When was the last time you saw Becca?' she asked.

'That was the last time I saw her.' Amy recalled the last words she had heard from her friend's mouth, before she fell into the road in front of the car: 'I don't want to be friends with someone who can't even run properly!' Amy pursed her lips as she wondered whether Becca had meant it when she said that. She realised, as if for the first time, that Becca had not visited her in the hospital, or even tried to find out if she was okay. What sort of a friend was she to abandon her when she was almost killed?

'Good.' Dr Grube's voice invaded her tangled thoughts. 'Well, we seem to be making progress, Amy.'

Here we go again, thought Amy. Dr Grube was always trying to get her to stop seeing Becca.

'This is a very positive step,' continued the psychiatrist. 'It shows that you are letting go and moving forward on your own. It could be that the trauma of the near-miss car accident has given you the wake up call you needed.'

The pink and orange swirly pattern on Dr Grube's dress was causing Amy's eyes to cross, so she turned away.

'I think you are letting go of Becca, finally.'

'Letting go of Becca?' *You don't even know Becca!* She wanted to scream at Dr Grube. The doctor was forever telling her that her friendship with Becca was unhealthy and that Becca didn't really care about her well-being. Perhaps Dr Grube thought the more she repeated it, the more chance she had of making her believe it; but Amy always thought Dr Grube was trying to brainwash her. She systematically rebelled against the doctor's words, believing that her parents had somehow conspired with the doctor to try to get rid of the one and only friend she had, so they could keep her locked up like some prized possession.

Amy shifted uncomfortably on her bed. She stared curiously at the unopened birthday present. As she did so, a part of her mind woke up, as if the red gift wrap was a beacon guiding her. Momentarily, her feelings of anger towards the doctor—and even her parents—lifted. She thought again about the last time she'd seen Becca. *Where has she been for the past few days? Why hasn't she come to see me? Could the doctor have been right about her all along?*

'I think it's about time I told you the truth about Becca,' said Dr Grube.

Amy wrinkled her brow. 'What do you mean?'

'You know how you're always reminding me that you are not a child anymore?' The doctor laughed.

99

Amy blushed slightly and looked at her hands.

'Well, guess what?' continued Dr Grube. 'I think that's true. The truth about Becca... I think you're grown up enough to hear it. You see, you needed her when you felt isolated, because of your circumstances. It's a good sign that she's disappeared now. She only existed in your mind... In your imagination.'

'What are you saying? She's not real? But...'

'You are growing up, Amy. You are letting go of your childhood imaginary friend. You are breaking free.'

Amy could only gape in disbelief.

'Aren't you going to open your present?' asked Dr Grube, snapping Amy out of her trancelike state.

The red package appeared blurry in Amy's vision, her eyes now full of unshed tears. In her heart, she felt a sense of loss. Becca's whole identity had been proclaimed null and void, all the times they had spent together were unreal. It was too much to take in. She lifted up the gift-wrapped package.

'Read the card first,' said Dr Grube, appearing as excited as a small child on Christmas morning.

Amy carefully placed the package on her bed and lifted up the yellow envelope. She opened it and saw a pretty pink card with the number 12 on it. Fancy calligraphy wished her a "Happy Birthday". Amy's brow furrowed. She felt anything but happy at the moment. Sighing, she opened the card and read Dr Grube's message. "Today is the start of a new beginning, the marking of a new year in your life. Time to leave behind anything that is no longer of value." *Becca*, thought Amy. A tear fell from her eye and made the ink on the card run.

Dr Grube picked up the birthday gift and handed it to her.

Amy fumbled with the pink ribbon, feeling awkward. All she wanted was for Dr Grube to go away, so she could cry in peace. As she tore away the gift wrap, she saw a book, titled: "Saying Good-bye to Karen" by Philippa Grube.

'I used to have an imaginary friend,' said the doctor. 'Her name was Karen. When I was slightly older than you, I wrote a book about her. She'll always be in my memory, and Becca will always be in yours.'

'Y... You wrote this?' Amy stuttered.

'Yes. I know why we create imaginary friends. It's partly because we think we are all alone and we need someone to listen to us.'

Amy flicked through the brightly coloured pages.

'I hope my book will teach you that you are never alone, Amy.'

Amy stared in wonder at the psychiatrist, and even began to think that maybe her dress was quite pretty after all. *Now I really am going crazy*, she thought to herself, as a smile curled on her lips.

Winter Blues

For as far back as she could remember, Adele had suffered, on and off, from a lack of motivation, feelings of anxiety, tiredness, mood swings, and a general sense of depression. Years ago, her doctor had thought she was run-down and advised her to take a couple of weeks off work. It didn't help. The following year, her doctor said she could be suffering from a virus, then the year after that he said she might be a manic-depressive. He prescribed pills, but they didn't work. Over the years, she had been for countless examinations and tests, scans and X-rays, all of which revealed that nothing was wrong with her. Finally, Adele was diagnosed as a S.A.D. syndrome sufferer: "Seasonal Affective Disorder".

'What does that mean?' she asked her G.P., bracing herself for the news that she had a terminal illness.

'It is quite a common condition these days, I'm seeing more and more cases of SAD syndrome,' replied Dr Ivory, as he typed something into his computer. 'It means that when there is less daylight, you are prone to feeling a little down. So, in the winter months you are not as motivated as you are in the summer. Looking back at your history, all your anxiety related episodes have occurred during the winter months. It's the lack of sun; that's what causes your bouts of depression.' He smiled sympathetically.

A sense of relief washed over her. There was nothing really wrong with her; well, nothing that a bit of sun couldn't cure.

'So, if I go on holiday to a sunny country, that should help?' she asked, thoughts of beaches and crystal clear blue seas filling her mind.

'Well, yes, that would be a short-term fix,' said the doctor, 'but you need to concentrate on finding something that will alleviate your symptoms all year round. With the British weather, this type of syndrome can be prevalent throughout the year, which is what makes it hard to diagnose.'

Adele wondered if she could ask for a villa in Spain on the NHS, a smile played on her lips as the thought crossed her mind.

'But it's not as bad as it sounds,' continued Dr Ivory, studying the papers on his desk. 'There are preventative measures you can try which have been effective for some of my patients. If you make sure you get out and about in the daylight as much as possible during the winter months, you'll find that you feel much better. Some people need more natural light than others. It's the way your brain responds to light. Artificial lighting, like the type we use to light our houses and offices, can actually have a detrimental effect.'

'But I work in an office,' said Adele, frowning. 'How can I get out and about during the day? And by the time I go home it's dark already.'

'Well, I can see how that could be a problem; being indoors for so many hours a day, going to work in the dark mornings at this time of year, and going home in the dark, might in fact be contributing to the way you feel. However, there are lights you can buy now: sun lamps. They are specially made so that they give out a natural light and can make you feel brighter.'

After returning from her G.P.'s surgery, Adele thought about what she had just been told and it began to make sense. It was all beginning to fit together like bits of a puzzle that had been scattered about but were now locking tightly into place. Although most people are happier on sunny days, Adele was aware this went much deeper for her. She began to notice that the sun had to be out for her to feel happy; and her symptoms were getting increasingly worse. Last winter she had become a virtual recluse; making up various excuses as to why she could not attend Christmas parties or meet up with friends. She had locked herself away at home, hardly venturing out even to the shops to buy food.

She told everyone who phoned her that she was sick with flu and that they should stay away in case they caught it too.

This year, Adele was determined to make a change; things would be different. The sun lamps which her doctor had told her about were very expensive, but she bought two; if they could stop her "sad" syndrome from rearing its head, they were worth every penny. She put one of the sun lamps in her bedroom, so that she could switch it on first thing each morning. The other lamp, she put in her office, to help cheer herself up during the working day. She slowly began to feel a bit better, as if she had more energy.

Adele began to read up about S.A.D. One Internet article stated that S.A.D. sufferers often feel more cheerful around Christmas time when streets and houses are decorated with lights of different colours. The lights and decorations in bright, vibrant colours, all help to lift their spirits and alleviate feelings of gloom and doom.

She bought plenty of decorations: gold, silver, red, blue, green, yellow; glittering balls, sparkling stars, and shimmering tinsel. Strings of multicoloured lights now decorated all of her rooms at home and even outside the house, to welcome her home after a tough day at work.

'But it's only October,' commented her friend and work colleague, Julie. 'Don't you think it's a bit early for Christmas decorations?'

Adele explained everything to Julie over a hot cup of tea.

'Well, now I understand your reasons, I'm all for it,' said Julie. 'I wish you'd told me about this "sad" syndrome earlier. I really believed you were ill last year. I must say I am disappointed that you were feeling so depressed and didn't tell me; it makes me feel like a bad friend. Promise me that in the future you'll let me know when you're feeling down.'

'I promise,' said Adele.

Julie kept a close eye on Adele throughout the winter months; concerned about her state of mind, looking out for any signs of depression.

Christmas came and went, and Adele was able to enjoy it with her family and friends. She felt like a different person, bubbly and joyful, full of life. When it came to Twelfth Night, she didn't want to take down the decorations. She asked Julie for advice.

'I think you should leave them up until the weather improves,' said Julie, thoughtfully.

'But won't that bring me bad luck?' asked Adele.

'I didn't know you were superstitious,' said Julie.

So, Adele left the decorations up throughout most of January, and far from feeling as if she had bad luck she continued to feel optimistic about life and was hardly ever down in the dumps; it was as if her S.A.D. syndrome had been finally conquered. Her whole life had turned around thanks to a few colourful strips of tinsel and bright Christmas lights; if only she'd known about this years ago.

Towards the end of January, Adele decided to throw a "Taking-down-the-decorations" party. She invited her family, friends, and colleagues from work. They all had great fun pulling down the hundreds of sparkling lights, trimmings, and embellishments, drinking wine, and listening to music.

'Your house looks a bit boring now,' commented Julie, as she left the party.

'Yes, it does, but I think the decorations have served their purpose for this year.' Adele smiled.

A few days later, Adele didn't turn up for work. Julie phoned her.

'I've got flu,' said Adele.

'Oh, I'm sorry, I'll bring you some soup later this evening after work.'

'No, don't. I think you should keep away in case you catch it.'

'I won't catch it,' said Julie, 'I've already had flu this year, remember?'

'Well, don't come over, Julie, I'll probably be asleep.'

Almost a week later, Adele was still off work. Julie decided to pay her a visit. After she had knocked at the front door two or three times with no response, she became concerned. She called Adele's number from her mobile phone as she stood outside the door, peering through the front window for any sign of movement in the house.

'I can't come to the door, Julie. I'm not feeling well,' said the little voice on the other end of the phone line.

'Have you been to the doctor? We're all worried about you at work.'

'Oh, don't worry, the doctor said I'll be fine in a few days,' said Adele, unconvincingly.

'What's wrong with you?'

'I'm just run-down. The doctor says I should get a bit of rest. I'll be back at work when I'm feeling better.'

'It sounds like this "sad" syndrome might have returned.' Julie's brow furrowed. 'I've been thinking that maybe we took the decorations down too soon.'

'No. I wish I'd taken them down a lot sooner,' said Adele, grumpily.

'But you're obviously feeling under the weather and it's been cold and grey these past two weeks.'

'I'm feeling low, but it's not because of my S.A.D.,' came the reply.

'Well, let me in, so we can talk about it.'

Julie sat next to Adele on the sofa in the lounge.

'It all started last Tuesday,' explained Adele, her head resting on her hands as she leaned forward, elbows on her knees. 'And I've been feeling depressed ever since.'

'Why? What happened?'

Adele sighed and leaned back on the sofa, still unable to meet her friend's eyes. She fiddled with her nails as she spoke: 'Well, as you know, I've had decorations up, including lots and lots of Christmas lights indoors and outdoors, for the past three months... and my sun lamps.

Remember I bought extra ones for the lounge and kitchen last month?'

Julie nodded and shrugged. 'What has that got to do with your mood? I thought they were supposed to help.'

'Last Tuesday I got my electricity bill,' said Adele, her face glum.

Michaela

The idea came to me after I watched a TV programme about rich Romanian gypsies begging on the streets of London and returning home to live in luxury houses. They made hundreds of pounds a day, apparently; yet they still begged on the streets as if they were paupers. I didn't consciously decide to take the route I took, well not at first. In fact, for a week or so after I'd watched the programme I joined in with the discussions at work, and disagreed with what the gypsies were doing as much as the next person, but somehow the seed had been sown. I remember thinking to myself while watching the programme: *I work hard every day and look at where I'm living, a poky flat mortgaged to the hilt, that I'll never be able to pay off ever!*

It was about a week after I'd watched the programme that I saw her. Michaela. She was so good at faking her poverty, I was almost in awe. She stood in the middle of the street, wearing rags, holding a paper cup in one hand, a walking stick in the other, wailing for all she was worth. I approached her and asked her name. 'Michaela,' she replied in a thick foreign accent, after I'd asked her twice, and she'd shaken her head in response to indicate that she didn't understand. Eventually, I'd resorted to pointing at myself and saying 'Melody,' and then pointing at her. The faintest hint of a smile and comprehension swept across her face as she said her name: 'Michaela.' The way she said it made it sound like a scrumptious dish.

She unashamedly held her paper cup towards me and I saw her mouth form into an O, as if she would start wailing again. I reached into my pocket, pulled out a pound coin and placed it into the cup. It made a clanging sound as it rebounded off the other coins she'd collected. She smiled, revealing a toothy grin, her teeth too white to belong to someone who lived on the streets.

As she hobbled away with her walking stick, a man in an expensive suit dropped more money into her cup. *That was so easy*, I thought, astounded. *Even after watching that programme, I gave her money!* It was almost as if Michaela held magical powers. *If it's so easy, maybe I should give it a try...* I heard those thoughts in my head but brushed them off. *I'd never have the guts*, came my inner response.

Two weeks later, I stood at the entrance to Russell Square Tube station in London, thousands of tourists, students, and workers, hurtling past at lightning speed desperate not to miss their train even though there was one along every minute. I'd taken the week off work.

When I'd gazed in the mirror before leaving my flat that morning I was unrecognisable even to myself. Inspired by Michaela, my natural blonde hair was now black; I'd bought a black wig and used my hairbrush to tangle it, so that it looked suitably unkempt. I used mascara to blacken parts of my face, and under my fingernails to make them appear unclean. I'd dressed in an old pair of grey jogging pants and a torn sweatshirt that was splattered with bits of paint—I'd been wearing it when I was decorating my flat the year before.

I bought a coffee from *Pret* across the road from the station, trying out my accent on the girl who served me. She was asking me what kind of coffee I wanted, but I kept repeating 'coffee' in an accent that I thought sounded close enough to Michaela's. One of the staff, who looked like he might be the manager (you know the type—wears a name badge with pride), said to the poor girl: 'Just give her a latte and get on with it, you've got customers waiting.' He surveyed me with a sneer that emanated hate and scorn. At that moment, I knew what Michaela, and others like her, must feel like every day, and part of me was glad she was screwing these people who would look down on someone based on what they were wearing. After all, under this disguise I was someone that man would probably smile at, even if it was a fake smile for customers who represented money to him. There are real homeless people—forget the gypsies who are playing the system—and it sickened me to think that this weasely man could get away with treating them like that, making them feel worthless. I sneered back at him.

I exited the shop, crossed the road, and kept walking until I reached the park in the middle of the Square. I saw a couple of tourists taking a photograph outside a red telephone box. An iconic London landmark. When I approached them, they backed away, as if I was going to shoot them. Sighing, I walked into the park, found a bench and sat down. The man who was sitting on the other side of the bench immediately closed his laptop, gave me a sideways glance and sprinted away. I had caught the look in his eyes very briefly; was it fear? Or plain intolerance? Whatever it was, it made the hair on the back of my neck stand up. I wasn't used to people treating me like a disease.

I drained the coffee cup, pouring half of it into the bin next to the bench. I then began to walk along the path, holding out my cup to people who were walking by, trying to imitate that look Michaela had given me. Somehow, it wasn't working. I'd been traipsing around that park for over two hours and had not collected a penny. My feet were tired, so I sat down on the ground outside the park gates. I took off my shoes and began to rub the soles of my feet. A shadow came over me blocking out the sun, and for a second I thought I was having a funny turn; but then I looked up and realised that the shadow was a man standing over me. 'Are you all right, love?' he asked. He was tall, wearing a navy-blue pinstripe suit. His hair was golden, highlighted by the sun; I could almost see a halo. He was very handsome. I blushed red beneath the black mascara on my cheeks. I almost forgot that I had disguised myself, and smiled at him a bit too brightly. He frowned and then I remembered what I was meant to be doing. *Typical that I should meet the man of my dreams when I look like something the cat dragged in*, I thought. Unconsciously, I swept my fingers through my hair, trying to impress him, but my fingers got caught in the tangled wig and I almost pulled it off my head trying to free them.

I realised that I was not going to win this man's heart looking as I did, so I held out my cup in resignation and tried to look sad.

He reached into his pocket and pulled out a wallet. He withdrew a ten pound note and handed it to me with a sad smile, then he walked away.

I watched him as he disappeared into a crowd of people headed towards the Tube station.

For the next seven days, I stood outside Russell Square station with my coffee cup in hand. I did quite well. Altogether, in one week, I collected three hundred and forty five pounds, and ninety eight pence; much more than I would normally earn in a week at my boring job as an office clerk.

I considered my options and decided to hand in my notice at work. The Romanian gypsies were on to something. This was an infinitely more pleasant way to earn a living; out in the sun, enjoying nature, instead of stuck behind a desk in an office, growing paler in colour as well as in heart.

When I ventured out with my coffee cup in hand that September morning I could never have guessed what fate was to befall me.

The day started out quite well; the handsome stranger, whom I had not seen since my first day as the fake Michaela, appeared on the scene, almost a month to the day I had first set eyes on him. And, he seemed to recognise me. My heart leapt. He gazed deep into my eyes when he approached me. 'Still here?' he asked sadly.

I nodded, pouting, trying to look attractive, though painfully aware that I was anything but. I imagined myself as Julia Roberts in "Pretty Woman". *Maybe this is my Richard Gere, come to save me from a life of poverty. Maybe he is a lonely, rich businessman. Maybe he feels sorry for me and wants to be my hero.* The fantasy thoughts whizzed around my head as he pulled a ten pound note out of his wallet and handed it to me.

I smiled, trying to look as solemn as I could.

He walked away and I desperately wanted to tear off my wig and run after him, explain that this was just a game.

That evening, I sat by the entrance to the Tube station as the newspaper vendors gave away the *Evening Standard* free, and the market stalls began shutting down for the day. I counted my "earnings". I'd taken to wearing a concealed money-belt because the amount I was making in a day wouldn't fit in the paper cup. One hundred pounds and twenty pence. *Not bad, I must be getting better at this*, I thought; then I frowned as I saw that one of the ten pence pieces was actually foreign currency.

I stood up and headed home on the Tube, gathering another twenty pounds on the way from unsuspecting commuters who were too weary after a long day at work to care about whether I was real or a fraud. As I looked around at the worn-out faces, some of the rush hour passengers falling asleep, I remembered the dead-end life I'd left behind, and I couldn't help feeling sorry for them. *If only more people knew my secret to instant wealth*, I thought.

When I stepped out of the Tube station at the end of my street, I saw the handsome stranger who had been at Russell Square earlier. Had he followed me home? A smile came to my face, but then a panic set in: what if he'd somehow found out he'd been duped into parting with his cash? Was that why he was here now? As much as it pained me to do so (as I really wanted to gaze into those deep, green eyes once again) I lowered my head and covered my face with the scarf I had taken to wearing to make me appear more like a Romanian gypsy (I'd perfected the look, in my opinion, after a month or so on the "job").

The man seemed to be following me. I kept walking along the street, and eventually arrived at my door. When I got there, I turned around, and he was about twenty paces behind me. I decided to sit on the ground outside the house, to make it look like I was going to sit there and beg.

He soon arrived at where I was seated, and reached into his jacket pocket. I thought he was going to take out his wallet again. Providence appeared to have had a hand in making us meet up again, and I assumed he wanted to give me more money. But instead of a wallet, he flashed an ID card.

'Melody Barnes?' he said.

My mouth fell open. 'How?' was all I could utter. I must have been in shock.

'Melody Barnes, would you accompany me to the police station? I have a few questions for you.'

The Game of Life

Vanessa knocked on the front door of the house she used to call home. She had asked her estranged husband Pete if he would be alone today, and he said he would; but she couldn't help worrying that his new girlfriend would be inside. Angie had told her, a few weeks ago, that Pete was seeing someone.

'I thought I'd better let you know.' Angie had phoned her one evening. 'John's just told me. She's young; a university student apparently.'

'What's she like? Is she pretty?' Immediately, Vanessa felt angry with herself for asking, for being jealous. Why should she care? They were married for four years and had known each other for at least ten years before that, but it was all in the past. She would have to try to move on—as he had done—no matter how impossible it seemed.

'I don't know what she looks like,' replied Angie. 'I haven't met her yet.'

Angie hadn't met her "yet". But she would be meeting her. Angie and John had been their closest friends. They often went out together on double-dates. Now Angie and John would be going out with Pete and his new girlfriend. Vanessa felt strangely obsolete, as though someone had swapped places with her, taken over her life, and even stolen her friends.

The front door opened. Pete stood before her. 'Hi,' he said, looking her up and down briefly, as one would a stranger. Leaving the door open, he disappeared back into the house without another word. She was left feeling very alone and unwelcome outside the front door.

Sighing deeply, she stepped into the house and closed the door behind her.

Pete was almost at the kitchen door, a few feet away. He turned to face her. 'I've put all the stuff that I think is yours in the living room. I haven't had a chance to go through the cupboard in the spare room yet, so feel free to take whatever you want from there.'

He left her standing in the hallway. It felt odd to Vanessa that this man, who was once such a big part of her life, with whom she had shared so many secrets, so many dreams, so many intimate moments, was now being so distant. Would he still be behaving like this if she told him that she had been having sleepless nights ever since the divorce papers landed on her doormat? Or if she told him that whenever his solicitor's letters arrived she would spend hours crying and wondering how it had all gone so wrong?

She had planned to tell him everything today, but he didn't seem the least bit interested in her and that made it all ten times harder. His new girlfriend was obviously more important to him now.

Vanessa walked into the living room and saw three boxes on top of the coffee table, neatly filled with the remainder of her belongings. They had agreed through their solicitors that she should go and collect the items this weekend. They never communicated anymore, except through solicitors.

On the top of the box nearest to where she stood, was a photograph in a gold coloured frame: a picture that Pete had taken of her on their first wedding anniversary. She picked it up. She looked really happy in the photograph, almost unrecognisable to herself. She couldn't remember ever being so happy, but evidently she must have been...

She put the photograph back on top of the box. Then she saw the *Scrabble*. As soon as saw it, she knew he must really want her out of his life. This was not part of her belongings, but he had put it in the box for her to take away, no doubt wanting her to take away all his memories of it at the same time.

She bought him this *Scrabble* game as a gift on their first Christmas together, when they had only just moved into this house. He used to own an old *Scrabble* set from when he was a boy; the board had fallen to pieces, and it was difficult to make out the letters on some of the tiles where they'd worn away over the years. Even so, that game had brought them together, literally. They enjoyed many games on that old set of *Scrabble* while they were dating. He had proposed to her after a game. When collecting together the tiles at the end, he spelt out on the board: 'W I L L Y O U M A R R Y M E.' She'd searched for the 'Y' 'E' and 'S' tiles to spell out her reply.

Vanessa recalled how much in love they were back then. Since then, of course, they had had many an argument over a game of *Scrabble*.

She opened the lid of the box and took out the board, laying it open on top of one of the boxes that contained her belongings. The familiar grid on the board brought back so many memories, almost an assault of reminders of both good and bad times.

There were good times. She sighed. If only he would talk to her, maybe they could sort things out. It just seemed so wrong to end it when they could have the chance of a new start. But it seemed that he could hardly bear to look at her anymore.

Perhaps she only had herself to blame for the way things had turned out. She had told him that she didn't love him, in the heat of the moment, during an argument about whose turn it was to take out the rubbish. Their arguments were always based on trivial matters, like who was supposed to feed the cat, or why he couldn't watch the news because she wanted to watch *Desperate Housewives*.

She hadn't even meant it: 'I don't think I love you anymore!' she'd said, but as soon as she said it she wished she could take back the words. It was too late. He had taken them to heart. Every day he would bring it up, and she would try to say that she hadn't meant it, but he wouldn't listen.

Several months ago, he said that he thought it was time they started a family, but that coincided with her boss offering her a promotion at work. She explained to Pete that the opportunity was too good to turn down, and they'd be better off financially. 'We've got plenty of time to plan a family; let's wait a couple of years,' she'd said. He took this to mean that she must have been serious when she said she didn't love him.

The arguments got progressively worse, and soon they were sleeping in separate beds. Then last month he filed for divorce. Now, here she was, collecting three small boxes of what was left from the debris of her marriage. She felt like walking out and leaving it all here. She didn't really need any of this stuff; there were just too many reminders of the past in these boxes.

Pete's voice startled her when he said, 'Would you like a cup of tea while you're here?'

Turning around, she saw him standing at the living room door. *How long has he been there?* she wondered. 'Tea would be nice, and perhaps we could talk?' She smiled tenuously. *He's still so handsome,* she mused, before she could get a grip on her thoughts. Sadly, she knew if she had only just met him today, she would have fallen in love with him all over again; fallen for those charms that had enslaved her once before. He still made her feel like a teenager... Even after everything they'd been through.

'Er... I think we'll leave the talking to the lawyers.' He began to walk away.

'Pete, stop!'

He stopped.

'Turn around, please. We have to talk.'

He turned to face her. 'I'll make you a cup of tea, but I'm not talking about any of this. Anything you have to say can be said in writing!' His jaw clenched and he appeared unable to meet her eyes.

She shuddered at the tone of his voice.

The sound of his footsteps slowly faded as he walked back towards the kitchen.

She looked at the boxes on the coffee table in front of her. Her mind was made up; she definitely didn't want any of this stuff now. It was better left in the past. Everything was stained with his imprint.

She picked up the *Scrabble* tiles in their green felt bag and was about to throw them against the wall, but then a thought struck her: *Anything you have to say can be said in writing*, he'd said.

Fine, she thought, *if that's the way you want to play it.* She emptied the *Scrabble* tiles out onto the board and found the letters she needed. Then she spelt it out for him in black and white: I A M H A V I N G Y O U R B A B Y.

She stormed out of the house, slamming the front door behind her. This action caused the floors of the old house to vibrate, so that the *Scrabble* board slid off the top of the box where it had been lying precariously, and the tiles fell onto the floor...

More books by Maria Savva:

Novels:
Coincidences
A Time to Tell
Second Chances
The Dream
Haunted

Novella:
Cutting The Fat (co-author: Jason McIntyre)

Short Story Collections:
Pieces of a Rainbow
Love and Loyalty (and Other Tales)
Fusion

Find out more about the author and where to buy her books, on her official website: http://www.MariaSavva.com

Printed and bound by CPI Group (UK) Ltd, Croydon, CR0 4YY

13/09/2024

01034268-0004